OLIVER BLACK

THE ETERNAL NIGHT

WRITTEN BY

HAYLEY MAE MASTERS

Young Author Academy
CREATIVE WRITING WORKSHOPS AND COACHING

"Oliver Black," published through Young Author Academy.

Young Author Academy

Dubai, United Arab Emirates

www.youngauthoracademy.com

ISBN: 9798341048140

Printed by Amazon Direct Publishing.

To my Family

Table of Contents

- Chapter 1 -

Something Unexplainable

It started on a Friday as odd things often do. My fifteen year old sister, Akira and I ate breakfast, got dressed and went to school.

My sister was three years older than me but she shared the same features: tan skin, freckles and jet-black hair. The only noticeable differences were a scar on her left eye whereas my left eye was blue. Whilst my other eye was the same green, like Akira's, lastly she was a girl and I was not.

At boarding school, HollowHead High, a dumb name for a school, Akira and I were known as the freaks. We didn't have the same lessons but during the break, we would always meet up at the taco truck at the front of school.

Today, however, seemed different, I couldn't explain it but something felt off.

"Oliver, over here!" yelled my sister from the other side of the fountain. The loud sprays from the gushing water almost blocking her calls for attention.

I hastily ran over to her but before we sat down on the bench, I noticed something. It looked like a pair of wings with a striking resemblance to those of a dove, but this was not a bird, it was something different. I looked around to see if anyone else had seen it but apparently no one had. I carried on with my day as best I could, which in fact, wasn't that normal.

In Maths, we had a test that we marked straight away, but I got most of the questions wrong, all but three. I blamed Mr Clarke, my maths teacher; he either wasn't in class or didn't seem to want help when you were stuck. In English, I was partnered with Demi Jones and Brooklyn Johansen, the popular girls who were quite nasty bullies. They would make fun of people; hurt them physically and the teachers would never seem to do anything about it. They would turn a blind eye to all their misdemeanours.

Demi had greasy-black hair slicked into a low ponytail and Brooklyn had short blonde hair with blue eyes as deep as the north-sea, cold and unpredictable.

The only lessons I enjoyed at school were Latin and Greek, which were both taught by my favourite teacher, Mrs Scythe. She had Hershey-chocolate-brown coloured skin that contrasted with the reddest hair.

Mrs Scythe's lessons were always fun and in my opinion, she was the only non-biased teacher in the whole school. I always loved it when she secretly taught us swear words in other languages and whenever she did, the looks on the girls' faces were priceless. I took great pleasure in reciting them in front of Akira. She had no idea what I was saying.

The day went on as a relatively normal day until lunch when on the speakers we heard the headteacher, Miss Olivia's voice booming through the corridors.

"Akira and Oliver Black, please report to my office at once!" Then just like clockwork, all the heads in the canteen turned to us and we got up from our seats.

"Miss Olivia," Akira greeted, pushing open the door to the office, "you wanted to see us?"

"Yes, I did," she nodded towards a man I had never seen before. His blonde, curly hair and big bright-blue eyes stood out even from across the room. "This is your uncle." Miss Olivia looked at him, "I never did quite catch your name."

The man looked at her and smiled, "Semreh, darling," he winked at her.

"Yes, your uncle, Semreh," she blushed, "wants to take you on a holiday, to catch up and to discuss becoming your legal guardian."

I looked at him suspiciously. It had been seven years since my mother had passed, seven years since we had been sent to HollowHead High, and this was the time he chose to meet us?

"Really?" I asked, "After seven years, what's made you decide to show up now?"

"Yes."

"During the middle of the term?"

"Yes," he repeated.

"Well, I'm sorry but I don't think I would like to go with you."

"I fail to see a problem," he said, confusion set in his electric blue eyes.

"It's been seven years since our mum passed away, you've never written or visited, and you expect us to go with you? Just like that, how do we know that you're actually related to us."

Akira nudged me in the side and Miss Olivia gave me a death stare but our 'uncle' just laughed, I didn't see what was funny.

"Well, you're a smart kid, but I assure you, I am related to you," he told me, ruffling my already messy hair, which I didn't like one bit.

"Well, what's your job? Or do you not have one?" I said with more than a touch of sass.

"Oliver!" shouted Akira, "Be nice," she turned to the man. "I apologise, he's just a little sceptical, he always is."

I stared at her in shock, I wasn't always sceptical, only sometimes.

"It's ok kid, I just want to spend quality time with you," he said, running his hand through his sandy-coloured hair, which I could tell he spent extra time on.

"We've looked at all the paperwork and everything seems to be in order. So, off you go, please, and get your things so you can head off with your Uncle Semreh," Miss Olivia said, waving us off with a flick of her wrist, shooing us away as if we were annoying flies.

When I arrived back at my form class, a lesson was in progress, everyone turned their heads and looked at me. I was thinking about just sitting down and joining the lesson but I knew the head teacher would just come to my class and drag me out so I headed to my locker and grabbed my bags. I heard everyone murmur, 'ooh', as I was leaving and I genuinely thought about cursing at them, in Greek of course, just so the teacher wouldn't understand, or maybe English would suffice, but it didn't matter if he did understand me, I would be leaving this wretched school anyway. What could they do if I did?

I headed toward Miss Olivia's office as slowly as I could. When I arrived, Akira was having a full-on conversation with the man, and she had the biggest smile plastered across her face.

"Oh my god, Oliver! Guess what?!"

"What?"

"Uncle knows really powerful people, he delivers messages and mail for them! He might know

Lana Del Rey or that guy you like to watch, Tom Holland!" She sounded really excited, so I gave her a small smile to cheer her up.

When we finally left, we headed into the woods, where we were welcomed by the thick trunks of the trees. As we continued to walk further, the forest seemed to become increasingly dense. We followed a path that led deep into the heart of the forest and I walked behind Akira and Semreh, who seemed to be talking as if they had known each other for years.

Akira was chatting with him regarding some nonsense about getting a haircut. I was still suspicious about this guy, he was supposedly our only remaining family that we knew existed, and yet he had left a five and an eight-year-old to fend for themselves out in the world. I didn't trust him as far as I could throw him and after thoroughly looking at him and inspecting his weighted abs and muscle tone, I guessed it wouldn't be far.

After what seemed like hours, I decided to take a closer look at the man, and after a thorough inspection, I stared at him in complete shock. I stopped walking.

"What's wrong Oliver?" Akira asked, looking concerned, "If you're tired, we can take a break."

I pointed at the man and queried, "What's wrong with your shoes?! They have wings."

Akira looked doubtful but she looked down and evidently saw a pair of small wings protruding from the man's shoes, they looked just like little feathery dove wings. Like those I saw back at school. Akira backed away from the man slowly, joining me a good six metres away from him.

He laughed and replied, "It's hard to explain, darling, I'll explain it when we get to camp."

"Camp!? I thought you said we were going to your house," Akira questioned, looking him up and down and hiding me behind her arms.

"I never said my house specifically, I said you would be coming to live with me, which I guess was a lie."

I turned on my heels and ran in the opposite direction with Akira trailing behind me. Suddenly, he appeared right in front of us, almost paranormally so we stopped abruptly. In a panic, we swerved and sprinted towards the other direction which soon became difficult because we were both out of breath. Immediately, we reached an invisible force that made us recoil spontaneously. Then I saw him approaching us from behind, it looked like he was levitating.

'Impossible,' I thought, then again he had winged shoes.

I tried to run at it again but it blasted me away into a tree. Akira ran over to me and helped me up.

"What is that?" she asked, she stood up on her tiptoes to try and see over the hill, but she saw nothing.

"Amazing, isn't it?" Semreh said behind us. "Hephaestus's work, give that man an hour, it's amazing what he can do."

"Hephaestus? Like the Greek god of fire, the blacksmith?"

"Yes, I was right! You are a smart boy." He ruffled my hair again. I thought good and hard about biting him.

"Well, I'm pretty sure Greek gods aren't real, only in stories and myths," I said with more than a touch of sass in my voice.

"Wow! See, this is why I've brought you here, darlings," he said to us.

"You mean in the middle of a dark forest by an invisible forcefield?"

"Ánoixe sousámi," he said, touching where the invisible force was.

"What language is that?" asked Akira.

"It's Greek, I think it means open sesame," I replied with confusion. Well... what good was that going to do?

"What's that meant to do, open an automatic door?" she said sarcastically.

"Try it," he urged.

With slight hesitation, we walked right through where the force field should have been and passed through smoothly as if we were a knife gliding through butter.

"If you're assisted by a god or someone who has already been accepted into camp, it will work."

"So you're a camper?" I asked, now curious.

"Oh no, I'm a god," he responded ever so casually.

"Which one?" Akira looked at him in awe.

"What's Semreh written backwards?" he quizzed us, I thought he ought to know it was his name. It's not that hard to tell us.

"Oh my goodness! You're Hermes!" Akira shouted, understanding the purpose of his quiz.

He bowed in mid-air theatrically and Akira knelt to her knees tugging my shirt so I followed her actions.

"But I wasn't lying about being related to you, maybe gods don't have DNA, it's rather complicated, you're demigods and we have been looking for you for a while now."

"Demigod, like Hercules?" Akira asked.

"Yes exactly, here we train you to understand gods and control your powers."

"POWERS! And why would we need to stay at a camp, what about an after-school club or a summer camp?" I asked.

"Well, not everyone actually possesses powers, only some of the strongest demigods or demigods with the strongest parents, do. Or if you train really hard and I mean, like climbing Mount Everest in your underwear, hard."

"Ok, good to know, why must we stay at a camp though?" Akira questioned.

"So, at camp, there's a lot of activities…"

"HERMES! Answer the question!"

"Well, sometimes there are monsters and creatures that try to attack, and sometimes if it's really important we send you on little adventures," he said, rocking a smile that eluded to, "You're probably going to die".

"You mean dangerous quests, don't you?"

"Well, statistically speaking, yes."

"Great! And I thought maths class would be the death of me."

"That's the camp," he said pointing down toward wooden buildings, made of dark oak, maybe.

"Camp what? Camp Olympus, Camp Demigod?

"Just camp, darling! Girls share a cabin to sleep, and the same with boys, and for meals, you have an allocated table, you sit with your half-siblings of your godly parent, Poseidon, Aphrodite, Hera."

"Great! So who is our parent?" Akira asked excitedly. This actually made lots of sense, well kind of. We had never known our father, and our mother never revealed anything about him when she was alive, we just assumed he died or they had split up or something normal like that.

"I don't know."

"Well, how do we find out?"

"How am I meant to know? I don't work here, I just deliver. Which I've now done, goodbye." And with that, he flew away dramatically.

"Well, that's great," I muttered under my breath.

"Well, let's give it a try and besides, we might find out who our dad is," Akira suggested.

We started to walk down the steep hill, but Akira kept slipping in her trainers and rolling down the wet grass, getting all dirty.

"You might need a shower." I tried my best not to laugh.

"What gave you that impression?" she asked sarcastically.

With that and the pent-up panic and frustration, we both burst out laughing, it wasn't that funny but we needed to laugh.

Upon finally arriving at the camp, we took in the breathtaking scenery. There was a dining hall with rows of tables, majestic mountains surrounding the camp, and a vast, serene lake.

Amidst this picturesque setting, we noticed an elegant woman conversing with a group of older teenagers, perhaps around eighteen years old. One of them caught my eye and spoke to the woman. As she turned around, a sense of familiarity washed over me, even though I was certain I had never seen her before. She had wavy auburn-coloured hair, stormy grey eyes, and was wearing an olive-coloured T-shirt.

"Hello, Oliver and Akira, I presume.? We've been expecting you."

I looked at her in shock, I suddenly recognised who she was, I had just finished reading a book about her, I looked at Akira who was already kneeling and looking down. So I did the same.

She smiled and said, "Don't be foolish, I'm not any more special than any of you."

"But you're Athena! Goddess of wisdom and war! You're a literal Goddess!"

She widened her smile and called over a girl who looked my age.

"Talia, over here!" she said and the girl hurried over.

"Yes Athena ma'am," she looked at the goddess. It was obvious she was more than a little in awe of her and maybe just a little scared.

"These are the Black siblings, Akira and Oliver, I entrust you to show them around," the goddess kindly asked.

"Of course, ma'am." She smiled and skipped closer to us.

"I'm Talia Rue Mallory, daughter of Nemesis, goddess of revenge." She extended out her hand.

"I'm Akira Beatrice Black, this is my little brother, Oliver." She pointed to me and shook Talia's hand.

I studied her features closely. Her brown hair was accented by a single blonde streak near the front on the right side. Her pitch-black irises were flecked with glints of gold, resembling highlights of white light but in a golden hue. Her complexion was deathly pale as if she were on the verge of passing out.

She showed us around the entire camp, even showing us inside the bathrooms. The whole place was too crazy to believe, the people, the places, the stories!

After an hour, she introduced us to a girl named Khloe, daughter of Hephaestus.

"She's in charge of making sure newcomers join a club," Talia explained, with a smile. Then she wandered off leaving us with Khloe.

"There's a lot of clubs here," she said in a thick Russian accent, "for example, this is Ari, Head of the sewing club."

I looked over at them and saw a girl around eight years old, prick herself with the needle and faint onto a boy sitting in a barrel so he fell to the ground. Akira looked at me and we tried our best not to laugh whilst the girl muttered "vlakas".

"Moving on," skirted Khloe hurriedly, scurrying off.

"This is Nova, the Prefect of the Zeus table and Head of Archery."

Everyone on the archery team seemed really gifted.

"Why don't you two try?" Nova said with a friendly smile.

Akira tried and missed the bullseye by an inch but we all clapped for her. When it was my turn, however, I aimed too high and accidentally shot a bird. So we tried something else.

"This is Lillian, Head of Makeup. I assume you want to skip this?" she asked us, eyeing Lillian up and down.

"Well, you never know Khlo," she said in a soft sweet voice, "they might want to try it."

She smiled at us.

I looked at Akira, I definitely didn't want to do this and Akira hadn't ever really been into makeup before, she would wear lipstick occasionally but that was about it.

We shook our heads politely and wandered off.

We observed some other activities, and all I seemed to be good at was sword fighting. So I chose that whilst Akira chose archery.

Even though it was our first lesson, we both came out feeling quite exhilarated and confident that we had chosen our activity well both showing a natural ability.

"I'm still confused," I said to her after we spent an hour in our clubs. "How do we know who our father is?"

"I don't know, but it can't be that hard to find out, right? Everyone else has found theirs."

We wandered off to dinner but we didn't really know where to sit. Everyone sat at tables that had a table draped with insignia representing their godly parent, there must have been about 2,000 tables in the room.

I saw Talia with one boy, she was talking nonstop whilst the boy looked utterly bored, rolling his eyes. I couldn't blame him, it looked like she had been talking the entire time. I noticed that Khloe and her half-siblings were scraping food onto a young girl's plate.

"Well?" asked Akira hastily.

"Well, what?" I queried.

"Should we go ask Athena where we should sit?" she continued.

"Uh, yeah sure," I considered.

We walked over to the long table at the front of the room and headed straight for Athena.

"Excuse me, Athena," Akira called over to her.

Athena looked up from her book to smile.

"I think I know what you're here for." She handed us a small jar. "Ambrosia and nectar, as it's your first time eating it, it should reveal your parent."

"Thanks," I said, as I raised the food to my lips. Just then, I noticed everyone watching us, and a chill ran down my spine. Despite the unsettling feeling, I took a bite and was immediately overwhelmed by a strange sensation, as if I were fizzing from the inside. I turned to Akira, who appeared as though she might throw up. Then, I noticed something extraordinary—something was gliding out of her chest, not breaking through but emerging smoothly. It was a lightning bolt. I glanced down and saw the same phenomenon happening to me.

"Akira and Oliver Black, offsprings of Zeus!" called out Athena.

The Zeus table roared whilst the others gave a small groan. I was looking around the hall and caught Talia's eye. She gave me a huge smile, what an absolute creep. Why was she always smiling? Akira and I walked down the steps and sat at the table next to Nova who clapped us on the back.

Akira and I just looked at each other, Zeus!

The King of the Gods was our father!

I stuffed my face that night but Akira hardly touched her food, probably because she thought if she did, she would throw up. It had been a very strange day.

That night, I unpacked my belongings and quickly fell asleep on the top bunk in the boys' cabin. However, I was jolted awake late in the night by a fierce thunderstorm brewing outside. It seemed my father was furious. A massive lightning bolt struck a nearby tree, igniting a spark. But as quickly as it had started, the rain extinguished the fire.

"Can't sleep, eh?" asked a voice from the other side of the cabin.

"No, does Zeus normally cause thunderstorms in the middle of the night?" I asked.

"No, only when he's really angry, like that time when I was ten and my friend and I took his underwear and hung it up as a flag," he laughed.

I tried not to but failed miserably.

"The name's Barnabas, Barnabas Wallaby."

I tried to shake his hand but since he was on the other side, I basically just rolled off the bunk bed, hitting the ground at the same time as another bolt hit the ground.

"What do you think he's mad about?' I asked Barnabas.

"I don't know, hasn't been this bad since someone put dry ice on the toilet seats when he came to visit."

I stayed up for the rest of the night wondering what he could have been mad about.

The next morning, I waited for Akira outside her cabin, and when she emerged, I was stunned. She had mentioned getting a haircut, but I hadn't expected her to follow through with it. To my surprise, she looked fantastic, and I was utterly amazed.

"Hey Oliver, look what the girls and I did last night," she smiled at me happily.

"You look great," I told her, returning the smile which seemed to please her.

"I don't know about you Oliver but I think I could fit into camp life quite nicely." I smiled. I also felt that this could be a new start for us, our first day was a good one.

When we arrived at the hall for breakfast, I noticed Athena there looking solemn.

"As some of you are aware, Zeus is furious, and we now understand why. He is being threatened by Nyx, who demands the return of her daughter, Nemesis. If we do not comply, she will plunge the world into eternal night."

'Okay,' I thought, it wasn't the best news by any means, but at least it wasn't Akira and my fault, by turning up at the camp, that made me slightly relieved.

I heard a gasp from around the hall. Athena cleared her throat.

"We will need brave and daring individuals to try and find Nemesis and bring her back to Zeus, any volunteers?"

A hand shot up from a few tables away but instantly went back down again, I tried to look over and see who it was but most people were asleep, that was odd...

"Well then, we will have to choose from you randomly," Athena advised.

To my side, a hand shot up.

Akira!? It looked like she was trying to bring it down with her other hand but was failing miserably.

"Akira Black," called Athena and Akira's hand flew down swiftly. It looked like she was about to fall off the bench so I caught her.

"What are you doing, you moron?" I asked her. "You've only been here for half a day! Are you trying to get killed?"

"I don't know what happened," she whispered back, "it was like someone else was controlling me."

I heard a giggle from the Hypnos table, of course, it was them, the children of the God of sleep and hypnosis, who else would it be? Who else could it be?

"Would anyone else like to accompany her?" roared Athena.

This time, however, I put my hand up. By choice, I couldn't let my sister go alone.

"Oliver Black will assist Akira on this adventure, thank you Akira and Oliver."

I smiled at her encouragingly but she looked terrified and truthfully, I was too, we had never had any training and we had just found out about the whole, gods exist literally the day prior. How were we meant to convince a goddess to come with us? But what if she was being held captive, then what?

"Pack your bags, Demigods, you will need to be prepared."

Be prepared, be prepared, geez! Great advice, we didn't even know where to start looking, we were about as prepared and ready for this as a giraffe on roller skates, we had no idea what to do or where to start looking.

As we were about to leave, Athena approached us to provide us with some weapons: a bow for Akira and a sword for myself.

"Be careful kids," she said, patting us on our shoulders.

Akira went to fetch her backpack and came back with some of her things piled up in it, a torch, a few spare clothes, water bottles and her phone. I added a few more things of my own. Athena lent us the weapons, a sparkling silver sword with a gold hilt and a beautiful bow with intricate designs. We said thank you but I was getting nervous, why did she think we would need it?

But before we were about to head, Nova approached us. "Try not to die out there," she said with a warm smile and handed us a few packets of beef jerky and a navy blue tent.

"Gee, thanks," I said, I wasn't looking forward to this 'little adventure' as Hermes put it, at all. I looked at Akira, trepidation lacing my voice.

"How in the world are we going to do this?"

As we turned around, we came face to face with a smiling Talia, and I couldn't help but jump.

"This is going to sound odd, really odd actually," she said, "but can I please come with you?"

I was shocked, why would anyone willingly go on a quest?

"Why didn't you raise your hand when Athena asked?" Akira questioned.

"I did, then I blacked out and woke up in my cabin," she explained, looking a little confused but still grinning like the Cheshire Cat.

I pulled Akira aside and discussed it with her, and we decided that an extra pair of hands may not hurt at all, or the extra knowledge about gods that could come in handy.

"Fine, but try not to dawdle," I told her, staring her down. "But why do you want to come?"

"Well, she's my mum, I would like to see her again," she revealed.

I had forgotten about that, I wondered how her brother, whom she was sitting with, must have felt.

"Well, yes. You can come with us but if you're too slow we will leave you behind," I said harshly.

She rushed over to me and gave me a huge hug, but I just pushed her away.

"Not a hugger," I told her.

"Oh sorry," she said whilst still smiling, I was seriously terrified.

We left spontaneously, with an awkward silence filling the air for the first few minutes.

"So Talia," Akira started, trying to start a conversation, "you only have one half-sibling?"

"Well, one that we know of, there might be a few more out there. But at camp, yes," she said clearly happy that the silence had broken.

"Can you tell us about him?"

"His name is Marcus and he's rather quiet. Come to think of it actually, I don't know much about him, he's never really opened up."

Akira nodded as if she understood, but I just walked in front of them. Obviously, he hadn't been able to say anything as he was either too intimidated by her smile to speak, or he hadn't been able to get a word in edgeways.

"Do we even know what we are looking for?" asked Akira as she stopped to take a rest on a rock.

"No, just anything suspicious I guess?"

"Talia, she's your mum, where does she like to hang out?"

Talia looked like she was searching back to her earliest memory. "She used to say she liked the restaurant, 'Demeter's Diner'."

She paused to think, running her fingers through her long hair. "In Sheffield, I think," she said, her black and gold eyes gleaming.

"That's not too far," Akira said, pulling out her phone, "it's only two and a half hours by train."

"But we don't have any money," Talia put in.

"Actually," I said, removing my backpack and unzipping the front pocket, "we do, thank you, Demi Jones." I smiled remembering how I had secretly slipped the money out of her rucksack. Served her right for always picking on people, I don't condone stealing but I just considered it payback.

"How much is this though?" Akira asked, "I'll look online to find the cheapest we can get."

I started counting, we had £20 to split between all of us, but for some reason, I didn't think that would cut it.

"It's £18.20 for one person, so for all three of us, it would be £54.6."

"So we don't have nearly enough," Talia said, "but don't worry, I have an idea."

"Was someone rude to you? Are you going to get revenge, like steal from them?" asked Akira.

"I mean, probably," I answered, "her mum is the Goddess of revenge.

She looked at us like we were from another planet, her smile not faltering in the slightest.

"We define our own paths, not inheriting our parents' identities until we decide to, I do not seek revenge!" she said, "Actually, what I'm doing is rather ordinary if I'm correct."

And with that, she headed off down the hill and through the forest.

- Chapter 2 -

The Wishing Fountain

We didn't stop until we reached our old hometown, where Akira and I were from, and even then, we had to beg Talia to slow down.

"Oh sorry, if you guys need a break we can wait for a while."

We all decided it was a good time to stop and snack on a bag of beef jerky and have a drink of water.

"Talia, where are we heading?" Akira asked, putting the empty packet back into her bag.

"Well, I don't know exactly but-"

"Hold on a second," I interrupted, "you don't know where we are going?"

"But I have a rough idea, I just don't know where it is precisely."

"We are not getting jobs," I said, giving her a death stare.

"Oh my gods, no, nowhere would hire you or any of us for that matter," she smiled, creepily.

When we headed off it took her about three minutes to apparently find what she was looking for. She started heading toward a nearby wishing fountain, one of those typical wishing fountains you throw coins into and make a wish.

But what was she doing?

We came to find out soon enough that she tied her hair up in a loose ponytail and stepped inside the fountain itself, she started to scoop up coins with her hands. I was pretty sure this was illegal so I did the only logical thing I could think of, I joined her.

Suddenly, we heard a piercing whistle.

"Hey! Get out!" It was Barry Prink, the local security guard. He had visited the school to give a lecture to the students on issues to do with safety and security and to ensure we knew the emergency numbers. I had fallen asleep during his lecture. I was hoping he wouldn't remember me.

Talia, still smiling, shoved the coins into her backpack, and walked up to Barry who was short and rotund in stature.

"Hello Sir," she said.

"That money you and-" He looked at me disdainfully, "Mr Black..." he did remember me, that was unfortunate, "are taking, isn't for sale. By that, I mean," he leaned in close to Talia's face,"IT'S ILLEGAL!"

My jeans were getting soggy so I stepped out and Akira gave me the 'warning stare' that mums do when they are upset at their children, the, 'I'm not angry, I'm just disappointed! Actually... I'm very angry' kind of stare.

So I gave her a sheepish smile and shrugged my shoulders.

"So give it." Barry held out his large sweaty palm with his demands for the stolen coins.

Talia took the coins out of her bag and turned away.

"Mr Black."

I handed him the coins and pulled a face at him, Akira pushed me away before Barry could retaliate.

"Great! Back to square one."

"Actually," said Talia, her smile growing wider and creepier, "we've got money." She shoved her hand into her black bag and produced a few coins, you thought Barry would have checked our bags.

For some reason, I started to smile as Akira managed to stifle a giggle.

"We had to get to Sheffield somehow, besides, I want to see my mother."

"You got quite a bit of money here, how did you know which ones to pick up?"

"I went for the pounds, obviously."

Akira started counting the money, whilst I was looking through the window of Dark Sphere, a video game shop I always wanted to go to.

I loved video games, I never had my own though. The first time I played one was when I went to my ex-friend Ishan's house and he let me play it on his PlayStation. I remember not wanting to go home and Akira having to drag me by the collar of my shirt. Suddenly, I felt a hand on my arm and I snapped back to reality.

"We started leaving without you," said Talia running, "we thought you were behind us."

I started to run after her, even though I had no clue where the train station was. Suddenly, I bumped into someone and clumsily fell over.

"Oh my gods, Skafos!" yelled a girl, helping the person I bumped into, up.

"Wait!" Talia said, squinting at them, "I know you."

The blonde girl shook her head, "No, you don't!"

"Yes I do, you're Hephaestus's daughter," she said looking at the darker one, who I noticed was blind, "and you, you're Aphrodite's daughter. We were all wondering what had happened to you, did camp let you go?"

I was confused, what did she mean by 'let you go' but I chose to ignore it and worry about it later.

The girl who Talia said was Aphrodite's daughter looked really pretty, truly beautiful. But after seeing all the Aphrodite kids at camp, I was sure all the Aphrodite descendants were stunning. It just about went with the territory of being Aphrodite's children. She had blonde hair, like most of Aphrodite's kids, swept into a low messy bun, bright blue eyes, just like the sky, and a pale complexion with darker patches, which I remembered as vitiligo.

"Yes, you do," said Hephaestus's daughter in a thick Italian accent. "No, camp did not let us go, we ran away."

"Why?"

"Look at us," snapped Aphrodite's daughter.

"Remember our meditation, Jane," Skafos said, placing a calming hand on Jane's shoulder.

Jane put on her headphones and started breathing in and out in a rhythmic pattern. From what I could gather, Jane wasn't a calm person, quite the opposite in fact.

"Aphrodite's daughter didn't quite fit the beauty standards and well, I'm blind, how am I meant to work in the forge? See? We don't fit in."

"Well, surely there was something else you could do, you don't have to follow in your parents' footsteps," Talia told her.

Jane took off her headphones and looked at Talia.

"You're different too, not like anyone else." She stared at her for ages, until Akira finally broke the silence.

"What do you mean? She seems quite normal."

I looked at her, she was normal enough but there was definitely something strange about her, that smile.

Talia cocked her head and stared right back at Jane. "What's so wrong with me?"

"It's that smile, it never falters. It's creepy and you know for a fact that everyone hates you because of it but you never stop because you're-"

"JANE!" Skafos shouted, almost as if she could sense what her friend was about to say, "No! She's just a child, you can't say that!"

Jane walked closer to Talia and whispered something into her ear, which made Talia's eyes glint in a murderous way. But just as fast as it happened, it disappeared.

"Thank you for that interesting information," smiled Talia and walked off, descending the train station stairs.

"What did you say to Talia?" asked Akira curiously.

Jane repeated to us what she had said and Akira gasped loudly and ran down after Talia, whilst I stayed and watched Skafos scold Jane until I figured it was time to go - which wasn't actually long after.

When I reached the base of the train station stairs, Akira was comforting Talia, who didn't actually look like she needed it, she was smiling, as always.

"Oliver!" Akira called over as I walked towards her, trying not to focus on Talia's creepy smile.

"Hey kids, this isn't a park," a lady behind the counter called to us, "you gotta pay to be here."

We showed her the money after I cursed at her in Greek. I then went up to the man beside her and paid for our tickets. She gave us a judgemental stare as we walked onto the train.

We hopped into one of the carriages, I was pleased no one else was sitting there with us. Well, until a young girl and a woman who looked just like her walked in yapping. (Great! Who doesn't love people talking nine to the dozen?)

Then a girl who had coal-coloured hair walked in, followed by a girl with dark purple hair, staring at us. I didn't know what that meant so I scooted across to make space for her, but she sat opposite us, with her glassy gaze.

Around halfway through the journey, a plump man came in with a trolley of food and asked us what we wanted. I eyed the pizza hungrily and I noticed Akira looking at the sandwiches. In fact, everyone looked like they wanted something except for Talia and the gazing girl, who seemed to be having a staring competition with one another. When the man left, we all dug in apart from the young girl, who looked like she was about to start crying. Then, you'll never guess what - she did! (I'm surprised she didn't cause a flood).

Honestly, we were all surprised and her mum leant right down to comfort her; bad idea if you're wearing low-rise jeans, and she just managed to sob out a whimpery, "The girl's smile is creepy," pointing at Talia, who's eyes just got wider with confusion, making her look like a killer porcelain doll. Akira used to have one and it constantly gave me nightmares. The girl started to weep even louder. Her mum turned her head, her long blonde hair whipping our faces as she started to scold Talia loudly. I could see Akira getting mad (she's very protective of the people she likes) and if I'm being totally honest, I was getting mad too, Talia didn't seem to care and just stared and smiled at the woman who seemed to get angrier. But then the trolley man came in looking worried.

"What 'append'?"

"This monstrous girl is intimidating my poor angel with that dreadful smile," she said pulling the brat closer (I'm not siding with anyone, but that young girl was so rude, imagine someone saying your smile is scary).

The man took a closer look at Talia and his gaze softened. "Look uhh, Miss. May you stop smiling for this little girl ere'?" He asked her politely.

But all Talia said was, "I'm terribly sorry, Sir, but I can't."

The woman started to yell again. Akira then stood up. "Excuse me, but you have no right to insult my friend," she said, her voice steady. "You're upset because she keeps smiling, is that right?"

The woman nodded, her eyes narrowing with disdain as she glanced at Akira. I could see the clocks ticking in her head trying to see where Akira was going with this.

"Well, maybe you should consider this, the world could use a little more happiness. And here you are, trying to make someone feel bad for simply smiling. Doesn't that seem wrong? Horrible actually?"

The woman shifted her gaze down to her shoes.

"And if we're talking about what's wrong," Akira continued, "you might want to reconsider your fashion choices. Your red turtleneck clashes with your lipstick and honestly, you've overdone it."

I stared at Akira, Wow! I didn't know she knew all that much about fashion. The lady took her daughter's hand and stormed out of the carriage. Akira stared at the plump man who laughed nervously and said, "Carry on," and then ran out of the carriage.

Suddenly, the noise of clapping erupted, I turned my head to see the girl with dark purple hair and dark blue eyes.

"Wow! Akira Black, impressive!"

We all stared at her, how did she know her name?

"Uh... How do you know my name?"

"Oh, I heard you guys talking," she smiled.

Talia stood up and stared at her intensely, a flicker of recognition spreading across her face, but she masked it well.

"We never mentioned last names," I said, hardening my gaze.

Then suddenly, the train jutted to a halt and Akira, struggling to stay upright, fell back and landed on me.

"What have you been eating?" I asked her, groaning, and shoving her off. Talia just held onto the pole and continued to stare.

"We should go," Akira told us, "it's our stop."

We jumped off the train before the girl could creep us out any more, I didn't know what was worse, her stare or Talia's smile.

After a quick look at Talia, I decided it was her.

"Who was that?" Akira asked nervously.

"My grandmother-" Talia's voice said unexpectedly, "...at least, I'm pretty sure it was."

"Who's your grandmother?"

"Nyx, the Goddess of the Night," Talia said, looking up at the night sky as if to explain to us.

I remembered learning about the gods a few years ago, no matter how much time goes by they will look the same. I honestly thought it was pretty weird that gods could look so young and be aeons old.

"Wait - you mean the one who is threatening our father?"

Talia nodded, "Yes, the one and only."

"And you didn't think to ask her about her daughter's whereabouts? Or anything about Nemesis that could help us?"

"I didn't want her to get too suspicious, besides, she's out looking herself isn't she, what makes you think she would know?"

"But why is she threatening our father? It's not like he knows where her daughter is."

"Nemesis means everything to Nyx, they're inseparable, sure Nyx has her other children, Thanatos, Hypnos, but there's always been a special connection between them, Zeus is King of the gods, so if anyone knows where she is, it's him and if he has information and isn't telling her she'll get mad, this is just her way of getting information."

"So she won't actually cause an eternal night?" I asked.

"Not unless Nemesis doesn't show up," she said as if it was the most natural thing in the world; as if a night lasting forever wasn't a strange phenomenon.

"Then we have no time to waste."

- Chapter 3 -

Secrets in the Woods

We ran for what seemed like hours and when we finally stopped in the woods, we were nowhere near Demeter's Diner. The thick trees seemed never-ending as if we were going in circles.

"We have to stop," said Akira finally, "we won't reach it today, it won't hurt for us to get a good night's sleep."

We all agreed and I went out to gather some wood so we could make a fire. I was glad to get away for a minute. I loved my sister, she was the best thing in my life but I had spent too much time with girls over the past few days and I just needed a break.

I slipped in between the thick oak trees looking for sticks that could be used to make a fire.

Suddenly, I felt a drop of water on my skin, I looked up at the stormy clouds. If we were ever going to need a fire, this was the perfect time. I picked up the last few sticks and hurried off to find the others.

As I made my way back to the makeshift campsite, the wind began to pick up, rustling the leaves and making the woods seem alive with whispers. Akira was already clearing a spot for the fire when I returned, her face set in determination despite the tiredness we all felt.

The first few drops of rain began to fall, and we all hurried to get the fire started before everything became too wet. Once the fire was crackling, its warm glow offered a small comfort against the darkness and the storm brewing above. Akira and I cuddled close inside the tent whilst Talia was tinkering with some sticks in the fire, the reflection of the blaze dancing in her eyes making her permanent smile look eerie in the flickering light.

Akira's voice broke the silence. "Do you think we'll find her?" she asked, her eyes reflecting the flames.

"We will," I said, "and then our father will be safe and the eternal night won't transpire."

Akira put her arm around me, "You're right, you're always right." She plastered a smile on her face and ruffled up my already messy hair.

I caught Talia's eye and saw her head cocked as she was seemingly trying to observe alien behaviour, all I could see in her eyes was confusion, had she never seen affection? Or was she just being her weird self?

I woke to the sound of thunder and sat upright. To my relief, the fire was still burning. But just as it appeared, my relief vanished when I didn't see Talia by the fire. Great just what we needed, a delay, it could take us ages to find her.

I looked down at Akira snoring softly, best not to wake her up. I clambered to my feet and dusted myself off, better start looking now. I grabbed my jacket and flashlight, my heart racing with worry.

The forest around us seemed darker than it was before, the shadows dancing in the occasional light. I called out for Talia, my voice echoing through the trees, but there was no response except for the distant rumble of thunder.

As I ventured deeper into the woods, my mind

couldn't help but imagine all sorts of terrifying scenarios. What if she had encountered some wild animal? Or worse, what if she had fallen and hurt herself? I pushed those thoughts aside, trying to focus on the task at hand.

Branches snagged at my clothes as I pushed my way through the underbrush, my flashlight casting eerie shadows on the forest floor. With each step, the knot in my stomach tightened. How could she have wandered off like this? Especially when it was us trying to find her mother. What was she thinking? Maybe she saw something, her mother, perhaps.

As the rain intensified, so did my determination. I cared as much for Talia as I did a white crayon on a plain piece of paper but she was crucial for this quest. As the rain fell, it soaked through my jacket, chilling me to the bone.

"Talia!" I called out, no reply. I called again, but still nothing.

As I ventured further, the forest grew darker, the towering oaks and twisted boughs forming an almost impenetrable barrier. The rain pounded relentlessly, and the thunder boomed louder as if the storm itself was trying to drown out my calls for her. I stopped for a moment, panting, the cold air biting at my lungs. My flashlight flickered, and I smacked it against my palm, the light stabilising just as I caught a glimpse of something in the distance, something white or was it blue? I wandered closer to it then suddenly, I face-planted into the mysterious white object, it was water. An uncomfortable sensation started to course through my veins, but I chose to ignore it.

"Ouch!" whimpered a small voice from behind me.

I spun around, the flashlight beam dancing wildly across the greenery until it settled on a small, huddled figure.

"Talia!" I gasped, anger flooding through me. She was soaked to the skin, her long hair plastered to her face, but she was unharmed.

"Talia, what are you doing out here?" I asked, my voice a mix of tiredness and rage. "You scared me half to death!"

"I'm sorry," she said, my torch illuminating her toothy grin, "I just needed to think."

"Well, couldn't you have done that back there?" I said pointing to where I thought our makeshift camp was.

She moved my hand towards an easterly direction and told me, "Not really, it was too loud." She looked at me like it was all somehow my fault.

I looked sheepish and I knew it, "I don't snore that loudly!" I muttered under my breath and she giggled. I looked up and what I saw surprised me. She was smiling, and not her usual creepy smile she always had plastered on her face, this one seemed genuine.

"Don't worry, it wasn't you."

I felt my frustration melt away, but only slightly. Talia might have been smiling genuinely, but it was hard to forget how she always seemed to cause more trouble than she was worth.

"Alright, let's get back to camp," I said, trying to sound more patient, "we need to be together, especially with this storm."

She nodded, still smiling, and took my arm as we began to make our way back. The rain was relentless, but it seemed lighter now that we were heading back together. As we trudged through the mud and underbrush, I couldn't shake the feeling that there was more to her midnight wanderings than just needing to think.

When we finally reached the camp, Akira was up, pacing worriedly near the fire. Her eyes widened with relief when she saw us approaching.

"Thank goodness," she said, rushing over to wrap Talia in a blanket, "what were you thinking, wandering off like that?"

"I'm sorry," Talia said again, her voice small. "I just needed some space."

Akira sighed, but her face softened. "Next time, let us know, okay? I was worried sick."

Talia nodded, her eyes downcast. I could see she felt bad, but it was hard to muster too much sympathy. We all needed to stick together if we were going to make it through this, and Talia's unpredictability was not going to help.

As we settled back around the fire, Akira looked at me, her expression serious. "We need a plan for tomorrow. We can't afford to get lost or separated again."

I nodded in agreement. "We have to figure out the best route to Demeter's Diner and stick to it. And we need to keep an eye on-" I looked at Talia as I stopped mid-sentence, so that Akira knew who I meant, although it was fairly obvious already. Talia looked up, her eyes reflecting the flickering flames. "I think I know the way," she said quietly.

We both turned to her, surprised.

"What do you mean?" Akira asked.

"I've been having dreams," she admitted, "and in the dreams, I see a path through the woods. It's like... like someone is guiding me."

Akira and I exchanged a glance. Dreams could be just that, just dreams. But given everything we'd been through, we couldn't dismiss them.

"Can you describe the path?" Akira asked, her tone gentle but curious.

Talia nodded. "There's a big tree with a split trunk and a river with rocks that look like stepping stones. If we find those, we'll be on the right track."

I frowned, trying to picture the landmarks she had described. It sounded familiar, but I couldn't quite place why. "Alright," I said finally, "tomorrow, we'll look for the tree and the stream but we stick together, no more wandering off."

Talia agreed, and we settled down for the rest of the night, taking turns keeping watch. The storm gradually subsided, leaving a damp, heavy silence. As I sat by the fire during my watch, I couldn't help but feel a growing sense of unease.

Talia's dreams, the strange occurrences in the woods, something was guiding us, but whether it was friend or foe, I couldn't say.

Morning came with a grey, overcast sky. We packed up our little camp quickly, eager to be on the move. Talia led the way, her eyes scanning the forest for the place she'd seen in her dreams. We walked in silence, the only sounds were the crunching of leaves underfoot and the distant calls of birds.

After what felt like hours, Talia stopped abruptly. "There!" she said, pointing ahead. "The oak tree."

Sure enough, a massive oak with a split trunk stood before us, its branches like gnarled fingers reaching for the sky. Hope surged through me. "And the stream?" I asked.

Talia nodded and pointed to our right. We followed her gaze and caught sight of the stream, its water clear and cold, with rocks forming a natural path across it.

"Let's go!" Akira said, her voice filled with excitement.

We crossed the stream carefully, the cold water splashing our shoes. On the other side, the forest seemed to change. The trees were denser, the air thicker. It felt like stepping into another world.

We moved forward, each step taking us deeper into the heart of the forest. The sense of being watched grew stronger, and I couldn't shake the feeling that we were on the verge of discovering something extraordinary.

As we continued, Talia's pace quickened. "It's this way," she urged, her voice getting more confident with each passing second. Despite my irritation with her earlier, I couldn't deny the growing excitement. Maybe she really did know the way, then Akira and I could meet our father, after all those years.

The forest grew darker, the trees taller and the foliage thicker. The path was barely discernible, and I found myself doubting Talia's guidance. But just as I was about to voice my concerns, we emerged into a small clearing.

In the centre of the clearing was an ancient stone well, its surface covered in moss and vines. Talia walked up to it, her eyes wide with wonder. "This is it," she whispered. "This is where she told me to go."

Akira and I exchanged a look. "Who told you?" Akira asked, her voice cautious.

"The lady in my dreams," Talia said, her eyes locked on the well. "She said this is where we'll find the answers."

My anger was noticeable, "And what exactly are we supposed to do with a well in the middle of nowhere?" I asked, my frustration bubbling to the surface. "This better not be another wild goose chase."

Talia ignored my tone and leaned over the well, peering into its depths. "There's something down there," she said, her voice filled with certainty.

Akira stepped forward, curiosity overcoming caution. She picked up a small pebble and dropped it into the well, listening for the sound of it hitting the bottom. But no sound came.

"It's deep," Akira said, her brow furrowed, "we need to be careful."

A sudden chill ran down my spine. The air felt charged with something unseen, something ancient.

"So, what now?" I asked, glancing around the clearing, half expecting something to jump out at us.

Talia looked at us, her eyes determined and her smile widening. "We need to go down there," she said, "it's the only way."

I opened my mouth to argue, but Akira cut me off. "She's right," she said, "we've come this far. We can't turn back now."

Reluctantly, I nodded. We found a long vine, sturdy enough to support our weight, and tied it around a nearby tree.

"I hope this will be long enough," I said as I helped Akira wrap it around her waist. She quickly slipped her legs over the side of the well, her movements cautious but steady. She disappeared into the darkness, and I held my breath until I heard her voice echo up from below. "It's safe! Come on down!"

I went next, my heart pounding in my chest. The descent seemed to take forever, but finally, I felt solid ground beneath my feet. The air was damp and cool, the only light coming from our flashlights.

Talia followed, and once we were all together, we began to explore the underground chamber. The walls were covered in strange symbols and drawings, telling a story we couldn't quite understand, I looked at them hard before someone's voice broke the silence. A woman's voice. That was strange, to say the least.

"I istoría tis Médousas" Ancient Greek, I noted. Though I didn't know what it meant, the only word I got was 'story.' I turned around but all I saw were statues; one in particular caught my eye.

"The story of Medusa," Talia translated for us, reading the writing on the wall.

"Correct!" said the voice again. "Rather an exciting story, did anyone turn it into a novel do you know?"

"Uh- I think so," I said, still studying the statue, a young boy with a school uniform on, a HollowHead High school uniform - our school uniform - the statue looked just like... no, it couldn't be, could it? The figure looked just like this boy who had once come to school with me, he had the same mop of curly hair and faint freckles under his eyes, but that made no sense, he had been expelled, he had left the boarding school.

"Hey Oliver," Akira said turning her head towards me, "doesn't that look like-"

"Zachariah Rigsby," I finished, "...yeah, it does."

I heard her gulp. "Maybe it's just a coincidence."

I looked at her, Zachariah had left school, went back home with a really weird woman and was never heard from again, even though it was custom to write a letter to school after a month away. This was no coincidence.

"Who are you?!" I yelled into the void.

"I'm Medusa, the girl gifted by Athena herself."

"Gifted? I thought it was a curse," Akira asked, covering her eyes with her hands.

Medusa chuckled, the sound echoing off the stone walls of the chamber. "A curse to some, a gift to others," she said, "Poseidon loved me, I didn't return that, like all men, his ego was hurt. He tried to hurt me, I prayed to Athena -"

I suddenly noticed a figure slithering closer, and Akira and Talia were both covering their eyes so I did too.

"-and after all the prayers and sacrifices she finally answered, she came and made it so no one could ever hurt me again. So you see, she gave me the gift of freedom."

"That's not what the stories say," Akira chimed, "they say you were cursed, Athena was jealous of your beauty."

"Does Athena seem like the jealous type?" Medusa cackled, "...Here."

I peeked for a second and saw a small piece of paper flying towards us, I reached up and caught it. It was a Polaroid picture of one of the most beautiful women I had ever seen. She had long dark hair formed into a plait and dark skin that seemed to glint in the light and the most beautiful long black dress that revealed her hips.

I noticed she was standing with two other girls.

"That was me..." she hissed, "...before, and my sisters."

"You had polaroids back then?"

"Listen, child, gods exist, demigods exist, and I think polaroids are the least confusing thing at the moment."

I looked at the photo again, her sisters were beautiful too, both wearing bermuda shorts and hawaiian shirts, you could tell who Medusa was. The myths were right about one thing, Medusa was beautiful. I passed the photo to Akira, then she passed it to Talia who said, "That's her, the lady from my dreams."

"My sisters-" she sniffed as she was remembering happier times. "Stheno and Euryale, they gave up their human lives for me."

I looked at Akira, would she do that for me? The thought of my sister sacrificing her life for mine made my stomach churn. As much as we loved each other, I couldn't imagine asking her to give up everything for me, she had already sacrificed her childhood to raise me.

Medusa's voice interrupted my thoughts. "They chose to stay with me, to protect me," she continued, her tone now mixed with sadness. "But it was a lonely existence, always hiding, always running from those who sought my head for glory."

"Perseus?" Talia suggested.

"Not just him, many others came looking, my sisters and I got separated." Her voice rose at this last part, as if imparting fault onto us, I know what it's like to lose homework down the side of your bed, I couldn't imagine losing Akira though, she was all I had left.

"I'm sorry that happened to you," Talia said soothingly, "but we really need to leave."

"Leave?"

"Yes, we are trying to find someone," Akira told her.

"Leave?" Medusa repeated. What was she doing?

"I'm afraid I can't let that happen, you see, you know where I live, you will tell the gods they will send people after me."

I looked at Akira and she looked back at me. We were screwed.

"We won't, we'll just leave and never return."

I started heading towards the vine and pulled on it to make sure it could still hold us, I noticed a small black beetle scurrying across one of the leaves. Suddenly, the beetle froze, a grey colour spreading across its body slowly, it fell to the ground with a soft thud, stone...

I put my hands up and retreated with my eyes closed. The air was thick with tension. Medusa's presence was overwhelming and I felt my heart hammering in my chest. The vine, our only means of escape, now seemed a fragile hope. My mind raced, trying to think of a way out of this.

"We won't tell anyone," I repeated, trying to keep my voice steady, "we just want to find her mum. Please, let us go."

Medusa's laughter echoed through the chamber. "Do you think I'm a fool?" she hissed. "Do you think I haven't heard these promises before? You can't leave."

I took a deep breath and tightened my grip on the flashlight. "Akira," I whispered, "we need to find another way out."

We looked at Talia who seemed to be scanning the room.

"Did you see any other exits in those dreams of yours?"

"No," she said, her voice cracking a little bit but her smile still remained.

"There's no other way out," Medusa laughed, her snakes hissing wildly, "either give yourself up to me or die fighting."

Talia started walking towards us, huddling us in a tight triangle. "Have you guys had any experience fighting before?"

"Not other than when we first came to camp, the hour of activities."

Talia slapped her face gently, "Just try your best."

Akira raised her hand and cleared her throat.

"How are we meant to fight someone we can't look at?"

The chamber felt smaller now, the walls closing in as we battled for our lives. Medusa's power was immense, and it was clear that Akira and I were panicking.

"Talia," I called out, desperation in my voice, "we don't know how to fight! What do we do?"

Talia glanced back at us, her eyes fierce. "Just follow my lead and stay behind me. I'll handle this."

I gritted my teeth. Sure she had more experience but I didn't like her being in charge, and it grated on me. But right now, we really had no choice. "Fine," I muttered, frustration bubbling up, "Just don't get us killed."

Medusa's rage was palpable, her voice a cacophony of anger and pain. "I will turn you all to stone!" she bellowed, her snakes striking out blindly.

Talia took a deep breath and stepped forward, her movements surprisingly calm and calculated, how was she keeping so calm? She grabbed a piece of shattered stone from the ground, its jagged edges sharp, and kept her eyes on the floor, avoiding Medusa's deadly gaze.

"Talia, what are you doing?" Akira asked, her voice trembling.

"Trust me," Talia replied, her tone steady. "I've trained for situations like this-"

(Who trains people to fight against mythological monsters and where can I find them?)

"-Just keep your eyes closed and listen for my instructions."

I squeezed my eyes shut, my heart hammering in my chest. The sounds of the chamber seemed amplified in the darkness. Every hiss, every scrape of stone sent shivers down my spine.

"Medusa," Talia called, her voice strong and clear. "You don't have to do this. We can help you. We can find your sisters."

Medusa's snakes hissed in unison. "You think you can deceive me with your lies?" she snarled. "My sisters are lost, just like you will be!"

Talia moved quickly, her steps sure and confident. I could hear the sound of stone scraping against stone as she found another piece of debris to use as a weapon. "Stay behind me," she ordered, "and keep your eyes closed."

Akira and I huddled together, she put her arm around my shoulders in a comforting way, our eyes tightly shut. The air was thick with tension, and every moment felt like an eternity. I could hear Talia moving around the chamber, her footsteps light.

"We won't tell anyone," I repeated, trying to keep my voice steady, "we just want to find her mum. Please, let us go."

Medusa's laughter echoed through the chamber. "Do you think I'm a fool?" she hissed. "Do you think I haven't heard these promises before? You can't leave."

Talia's voice was calm but firm. "We're not lying, Medusa, we know the gods have wronged you. We can help you find peace."

Medusa's laughter was bitter. "Peace? There is no peace for me. Only eternal suffering!"

As Talia edged closer to Medusa, the gorgon's eyes narrowed in on her. "And you, girl, with that permanent, fake smile," Medusa spat, "I don't know how you can expect anyone to love you when you so clearly hate yourself."

Talia froze, her grip tightening on the stone. She took a deep breath, her voice trembling with a mix of anger and sorrow. "I don't hate myself,

Medusa. I've been through things you can't imagine, but I don't hate myself."

Medusa's snakes hissed and writhed. "Do you think pity will save you? You think you can talk your way out of this?"

Talia's voice softened, a note of empathy cutting through the tension. "I'm not here to fight you. I understand pain and loneliness. I've spent my life trying to protect others because I know what it feels like to be abandoned."

Medusa's laughter was cold and hollow. "And what good has it done you? Look at you, hiding behind that smile, pretending everything's fine when it's not."

Talia's eyes filled with tears, her smile looking like it might fade for a moment, but of course it didn't.

"You're right! It's not fine but I still believe in helping others. I still believe in love, despite everything."

Medusa's gaze bore into Talia as if searching for the truth in her words. "Love? Do you really think you understand love?"

Talia's tears spilled over, her voice breaking. "Yes, I do. Love is what keeps me going, what gives me strength. It's what brought us here, to find my mother, to help her, to help you if you would only let us."

For a moment, the chamber was silent except for the distant rumble of thunder. Medusa seemed to falter, her snakes quieting.

"Love..." Medusa whispered, her voice barely audible, "I loved once, and it brought me nothing but pain."

Talia took a cautious step closer, her pitch-black eyes covered by her hand. "Then let us help you find peace. Let us help you find your sisters. You don't have to be alone anymore."

For a moment, Medusa looked hopeful but then I heard a loud smack and someone falling to the floor. At first, I thought it was Medusa but then I took a quick glance and saw Talia groping for her blade and Medusa moving closer...

- Chapter 4 -

The Fight with Medusa

I could feel the cold dread creeping over me, threatening to paralyse me, but Talia's words echoed in my mind, reminding me that we were here for a purpose greater than ourselves.

"Akira," I whispered urgently, "we have to do something."

Akira nodded, her face pale but determined. "I know, we can't let her die."

Summoning all my courage, hoping to distract her, I shouted, "Hey, Medusa! over here!" my voice cracking with fear.

Medusa's head snapped towards me, her snakes writhing in anger. "Foolish boy," she spat, "do you think you can save her?"

Talia, taking advantage of the distraction, managed to grab her blade and scramble to her feet. Her voice, though shaky, held a note of defiance.

"We're not here to fight you, Medusa. We're here to help you."

As Medusa's gaze fell upon us, her expression unreadable, Talia stepped forward with an outstretched hand. "We can find your sisters. We can end this cycle of pain and loneliness. But you have to let us go."

Medusa's eyes flickered with a mixture of suspicion and longing, but her hardened expression remained unchanged. "And if I let you go, what guarantee do I have that you won't betray me?"

Akira, her voice steady despite the fear in her eyes, stepped closer. "Because we understand loss. We know what it's like to be alone. We won't betray you, Medusa, we swear it."

Medusa's gaze softened briefly, but then she shook her head. "No," she said firmly, "I can't take that risk."

Before any of us could react, Medusa struck out with a swift motion, hitting Talia with the back of her hand and sending her sprawling to the ground again. Talia's blade clattered away, rendered useless.

"Talia!" Akira screamed, rushing to her side, but Medusa wasn't finished. With a sudden, vicious motion, she turned her attention to Akira and me, her eyes glowing with an intense, green light which was mesmerising but knowing that we mustn't look into her illuminated eyes I quickly looked away. I felt a surge of anger and fear rise within me as Medusa's snakes snapped and hissed. Without thinking, I lunged forward, grabbing a nearby rock and hurling it directly at Medusa. It struck her shoulder, but she barely flinched.

She swerved her head towards me, but I looked away whilst Akira was helping Talia to her feet, I reached for my sword and pointed it towards Medusa.

The air crackled with apprehension as Medusa's gaze hardened, her snakes writhing with renewed fury. My heart pounded in my chest as I stood frozen in place, my mind racing with fear and uncertainty. Behind me, Akira's wide eyes mirrored my own terror, her hands trembling at her sides.

"We have to do something," I stammered, my voice barely above a whisper as I glanced desperately at Akira.

Akira, her face pale but determined, nodded in agreement. "Yeah, we can't just stand here," she muttered, her voice wavering with uncertainty.

But as Medusa advanced, her movements swift and deadly, I felt a surge of panic welling up inside me. My limbs felt heavy and unresponsive, my mind clouded with a paralysing fear that threatened to consume me whole.

Talia, recognizing our fear, fought valiantly to defend us, but it was clear that we were outmatched. Without the skills or experience to match Medusa's ferocity, Akira and I stumbled backward, tripping over our own feet in a lousy attempt to evade her wrath.

Panic surged through me as I felt the searing pain of Medusa's strike, her serpent's fangs sinking into my shoulder with merciless precision. I cried out in agony, my vision swimming as I struggled to remain upright.

Akira, her breath coming in ragged gasps, could only watch in horror as I was attacked before her eyes. The weight of her own helplessness bore down on her like a leaden weight, suffocating her with a sense of despair.

But even in the face of overwhelming odds, a spark of defiance flickered within me. With a newfound resolve born of desperation, I refused to give in to despair, I wouldn't allow myself to die in front of Akira, she gave up her life to raise me, I couldn't let everything she did be for nothing, especially not in front of Talia. Clinging to Akira for support, I stumbled forward, my movements clumsy but determined.

As the chaos unfolded around us, Talia sprang into action with a desperate plan forming in her mind. Ignoring the pain from her earlier blow and the steady flow of blood trickling down the back of her head, she scrambled to her feet and searched frantically for something, anything, that could help us turn the tide of battle.

And then, as if by some stroke of luck, her gaze fell upon the sword Athena lent us, I was beginning to understand why she thought we needed it. She picked it up from the damp stone floor, its surface gleaming in the dim light of the chamber. With a surge of hope, she snatched it up and turned it towards Medusa, her hands trembling with adrenaline-fuelled determination. But it was evident Medusa knew what Talia was planning, however, we had learned Talia was unexpected, she quickly threw the sword over to us, which seemed rather dangerous but I didn't comment, Medusa's head quickly swerved round to face us.

"Oliver, Akira, look away!" Talia shouted, her voice ringing out above the din of battle.

With a sinking feeling in my gut, I obeyed, averting my gaze as I clung to Akira's side, my heart pounding with a mixture of dread and anticipation. Everyone was still for a moment, or at least I didn't hear anyone move. Then Medusa's snakes suddenly got louder as if they were coming closer so I started to feel around for the sword. I grabbed it by the hilt and slowly opened my eyes just a little. I saw Talia peeking too, she gave me a slight nod and I swung the sword, hoping to maybe cut off her head like in the ancient tales or maybe, I wasn't sure what I was thinking, I wasn't thinking.

I heard the sharp crack of shattering stone, followed by a deafening silence that seemed to stretch on for eternity. With a sense of dread, I slowly turned my gaze back towards the scene unfolding before me.

And there, standing frozen in place, was Medusa - a statue of stone, her features twisted in a grotesque expression of rage and agony. The sun was shining off the sword at just the right angle so the light hit directly at her eyes.

For a moment, we stood in stunned silence, the weight of what had just transpired hanging heavy in the air.

"We have to finish this," Talia said, her voice resolute despite the tremor of uncertainty that lingered beneath the surface. She looked directly at me, which sent a shiver down my spine. I still didn't trust her. Something about her was off, starting with that smile. Everyone we had met along the way had said that smile was strange, I knew it, they knew it, and even Akira knew it even though she was too polite to say so. It was just a gut feeling something was off, I didn't know what it was.

"Do you want to do it?" she asked me.

"Pardon?"

"Do you want to finish it?" she repeated.

I just stared at her, did I? I mean not really, I wasn't sure I wanted to kill someone at twelve years old, even if they did try to murder us, on the other hand, it needed to be done, right?

I mean it would give me an edge, bragging rights, defeating Medusa and being the new kid at camp. It couldn't do me any harm if the other kids thought I was strong and unafraid (little would they know I was literally bricking it).

"What about Akira?" I looked over at her expectantly, hoping that she would say yes, but she just shook her head.

"Oh- uh, sure, okay, can't be that hard right?" I said, fumbling with the sword in my hands.

I tightened my grip on the sword and tried to encourage myself, I brought it down upon her head and the stone clattered into hundreds of small pieces.

I couldn't shake the feeling that our journey with her was far from over and the true danger had only just begun...

Akira, sensing my discomfort, placed a reassuring hand on my shoulder. "Are you okay, Oliver?"

I nodded, though my gaze remained fixed on Talia. "Yeah, I'm fine. Just... tired."

Akira gave Talia a grateful nod. "Thank you, Talia. We wouldn't have made it without you."

Talia's smile widened, but I could see the calculation behind her eyes. "We should rest, we'll need our strength for the journey ahead."

Akira nudged my ribs, pressing me to say something, "Yeah, thanks -" But in my mind I was thinking there's more behind this girl. "Maybe we are better not following your dreams in the future."

We climbed back up the vine, which took longer than it should have. As we settled down to rest, I couldn't shake the unease that gnawed at me. I loved my sister more than anything, and I would do whatever it took to protect her, and that meant keeping a close eye on Talia, no matter how much she tried to prove herself.

In the stillness of the aftermath, Akira tended to my wounds with gentle hands, I made a silent vow, I would keep my guard up, for Akira's sake and for mine. The battle with Medusa was over, but the real fight, the fight for trust, for survival, had only just begun and I didn't even trust Talia as much as I trusted Hermes when I first met him.

As I lay there, the ache from my wounds throbbing in the dim light, I couldn't help but glance over at Talia. She was tending to her own injuries with a calm efficiency that seemed almost inhuman still with that unsettling grin. Every now and then, she'd catch me looking and make her smile wider. It made my skin crawl.

Akira, always the compassionate one, seemed oblivious to the tension. "Here, let me help you with that," she offered, moving to assist Talia with a particularly nasty cut on her arm.

Talia hesitated, then nodded gratefully. "Thanks, Akira, you're too kind, but I'm fine, really."

'Way too kind,' I thought bitterly. Too trusting. As Akira carefully bandaged her own wounds, I couldn't shake the nagging feeling that we were making a mistake. Trusting Talia might have saved us from Medusa, but what if it led us into even greater danger?

The night wore on, and despite the exhaustion that pulled at my eyelids, sleep refused to come. My mind was a whirlpool of doubts and fears, each one dragging me deeper into uncertainty. I glanced at Akira, now asleep beside me, her face serene despite everything we'd been through. I loved her more than anything in this world, and I would do whatever it took to keep her safe. I didn't care what would happen to me, as long as she was safe.

As I was trying to sleep, Talia's voice broke the silence. "Look at the stars."

I did, they looked the same as always, white dots in the sky. "Yeah, what about them?"

"Just look closely, you can see so many constellations: Cassiopeia, Cepheus, Draco, Ursa Major, and Ursa Minor."

I looked up again and studied the stars more closely when I noticed the star sign Aquarius that lit up the night sky in February. I never paid much attention to stars before, not that I didn't think they were beautiful on a clear night but I've never really shown an interest in astronomy.

Talia looked at me like I was a new species she was trying to figure out. Her eyes sparkled with a mixture of amusement and curiosity as she looked at me. "Oh, but they are so much more than just balls of gas or white dots in the sky, Oliver. They hold stories, myths, and legends that have captivated humanity for centuries."

Her voice took on a dreamy quality as she began to weave tales of the ancient Greeks, their gods, and the heroes who dared to challenge them. "You see, the stars are like a tapestry, each constellation a thread in the design of the universe. Within that tapestry lie stories of love, betrayal and power."

She gestured towards the constellation of Orion, his mighty figure dominating the night sky. "Take Orion, for example. In Greek mythology, he was a great hunter, feared by all creatures of the earth. But even the mightiest of hunters can be brought low by fate, as Orion discovered when he fell in love with the beautiful Artemis."

As Talia spoke, her passion for the stories of old was palpable, her words painting vivid pictures of gods and monsters locked in an eternal struggle for power. "And then there's the story of Perseus and the Gorgon, Medusa, you obviously know her," she continued, her gaze lingering on the constellation of Perseus, his sword held high in defiance. "Perseus was a hero, brave and cunning, who dared to face the monstrous Medusa and emerged victorious, using a polished shield as a mirror to avoid her deadly gaze."

I listened intently as Talia spun her tales, each one more captivating than the last, as she told the stories I could imagine I was there, seeing everything. In her words, I could hear echoes of the ancient storytellers who had come before her, their voices carried in the wind like whispers from the past. And as I gazed up at the stars, their light shimmering in the darkness, I began to understand why Talia loved them so much. For her, the stars were more than just dots, they were windows into a world of magic and wonder, where anything was possible.

And in that moment, as I lost myself in the stories she was telling, I felt a sense of awe wash over me, connecting me to something bigger than I could ever be a part of.

As the night wore on and the tales came to an end, I found myself seeing the stars in a new light. No longer just distant specks in the sky, but symbols of hope and inspiration, guiding us on our journey through the darkness. And though the road ahead was fraught with danger and uncertainty, I knew that as long as we had the stars to light our way, we would never be truly alone.

"I told you," Talia sighed tilting her head up to the sky, "the stars, they're amazing, make sure to tell your school friends this."

I looked at her, her pale face, almost white in the moonlight. I didn't want to tell her that Akira was my only friend and maybe Barnabas from the cabin, I wasn't sure. I wasn't good at making friends or knowing if I was someone's friend.

"Yeah, definitely. If I'm allowed back there."

She looked at me, "What do you mean?"

"We are at camp now, are we allowed to go back to normal school?"

"Yes, but most people stay at camp, it has all normal lessons, Maths, English and all that."

"And some things not so normal," I finished off for her.

"Yeah," she laughed, "but it's all good fun honestly, and it gives you a better chance of connecting with people."

As the night wore on and sleep continued to elude me, I found myself staring up at the stars, their distant light offering little comfort in the face of the doubts that plagued my mind, and as

Talia's voice broke the silence once more, urging me to look closer, I couldn't help but wonder what secrets lay hidden behind her mysterious smile.

When we awoke the next day, we started heading off straight to Demeter's Diner, but we knew our journey to Demeter's Diner would be fraught with challenges and uncertainties, each step a testament to our determination to push forward despite the odds stacked against us.

The forest loomed around us, its ancient trees casting long shadows that seemed to stretch endlessly into the depths of the forest. With every rustle of leaves and creak of branches, the wilderness seemed to come alive, a living, breathing entity that watched our every move with silent scrutiny.

As we ventured deeper into the forest, the path became increasingly treacherous, the undergrowth thickening with each passing step. Twisted roots snaked across the forest floor like gnarled fingers, threatening to trip us up at every turn. Yet, despite the obstacles that lay in our path, we pressed on, all of us being hyper-aware, every time so much as a leaf fell.

With every passing hour, the sun dipped lower in the sky, casting long shadows that stretched out before us like ominous omens of the trials to come. The air grew thick with the scent of earth and pine, a heady mixture that filled our lungs with each breath.

"Let's stop for lunch," Akira finally suggested.

We took out some beef jerky from her blue backpack and sat down on a mossy log.

"Do you know how far away we are from the diner?" I asked Talia, hoping that when we got there they would have something more appetising than beef jerky to eat.

"I think we are close, I'm not sure though. I haven't been here in years."

I looked at her, confused, why were we following someone who didn't actually know where they were going? But as my brain processed it, I didn't see a better option, we had less of an idea than she did, so I followed behind her, still confused.

- Chapter 5 -

Demeter's Diner

As we finally emerged from the dense forest, a small wooden cabin came into view, nestled in a clearing like a hidden gem. It looked old and quaint, with a charming rustic exterior that made it seem like a cosy, isolated place to hang out. The wooden beams were aged and weathered, but the structure stood strong, exuding an inviting warmth despite its remote location.

"Is this it?" I asked, glancing at Akira and Talia. The cabin seemed far too small to be the bustling pub we had been anticipating.

"Yes," Talia replied with a nod, "it might not look like much from the outside, but you'll see."

As we approached, the sounds of laughter and chatter became loud, filtering through the walls of the cabin. I exchanged a curious look with Akira before pushing the creaky wooden door open.

Stepping inside, I was immediately struck by the stark contrast to the exterior. The interior of the cabin was expansive, stretching far beyond what seemed possible from the outside. The ceiling soared high above us, adorned with intricate wooden carvings and glowing lanterns that cast a warm, golden light.

The place was bustling with activity. Long wooden tables filled the space, each one crowded with people of all ages and backgrounds. Some were eating hearty meals, while others were engaged in animated conversations or games. The aroma of freshly baked bread and savoury dishes wafted through the air, mingling with the sounds of clinking cutlery and lively chatter.

"Welcome to Demeter's Diner," a nearby waiter said with a warm smile, her rich eyes twinkling with pride, "it's a place of refuge and community for those who know where to find it."

"Thanks... can we get a table?" I asked.

"Of course," she replied, leading us through the bustling room to a cosy corner table. As we settled in, I couldn't help but marvel at the intricate details of the diner. The wooden walls were lined with shelves holding ancient books and artefacts, and tapestries depicting mythological scenes hung between the lanterns, their colours vibrant and stories captivating.

Akira looked around with wide eyes, taking in the lively atmosphere. "This place is incredible," she whispered, her face lighting up with wonder.

Talia looked around too, a small smile playing on her lips, not her normal toothy grin but a small sweet smile.

A server appeared with menus, offering us a selection of mouthwatering bakery items. We scanned the options, each one sounding more tempting than the last.

We placed our orders whilst the server nodded, jotting down our choices. "Excellent selections. Your pastries will be ready shortly."

As we waited for our food, which wasn't very long, we watched the other patrons, their faces reflecting a mix of joy and relief. The sense of community and camaraderie in the diner was transparent, and it was clear that this place was a sanctuary for many.

Our food arrived, and we dug in. The flavours were rich and comforting, each bite more delicious than the last. As we ate, I couldn't help but feel a sense of calm wash over me. This place, with its warmth and welcoming atmosphere, was exactly what we needed after our long journey.

Leaning back in my chair, I looked up at the high ceiling, the lanterns casting a gentle glow. With that, we settled in, grateful for the refuge Demeter's Diner provided. For now, we had found a place of peace, and that was enough, Demeter would just have to wait.

"Oliver! Wake up," Akira was shaking me, "we have to find Demeter."

I sat up with a jolt as I shook off the drowsiness. I realised we were still seated at our table in Demeter's Diner, surrounded by the comforting scent of freshly baked pastries and the lively chatter of other groups of customers.

Akira's urgent voice cut through the haze of sleep, pulling me back to reality. "She's in the kitchen," Akira said, her eyes wide with determination.

With a renewed sense of purpose, we rose from our seats and made our way through the bustling diner towards the kitchen area. The savoury scent of cooking filled the air as we approached, mingling with the warm, golden light that spilled out from the doorway.

Pushing open the door, we stepped inside to find ourselves in the heart of the kitchen. Straight away, I knew something was wrong. There was only one person in there, a beautiful woman with chestnut brown hair, tied in a low ponytail and deep brown eyes full of warmth.

"Hi, Miss?" Akira said and the woman turned around looking straight at us.

"Hello my lovelies, anything I can do for you?"

"Is Nemesis here?" I asked, getting straight to the point.

The woman looked at me, confused for a moment.

"Which one?"

"What do you mean 'which one'?"

She looked at us and laughed.

"There's so many dear, it's a very popular name at the moment."

We all looked at each other, did gods have last names?

"The Goddess of revenge?"

Demeter's face hardened, and her eyes narrowed.

"She used to hang out here a lot," Talia told her, "she's missing."

I heard Demeter snort and try to hide a small sly smile. "Well, she ain't here, she's banned for life."

"Why?"

"She caused quite a stir last time she was here," Demeter replied, her voice carrying an edge of frustration, "disrupted the peace of this place, stirring up conflicts among the patrons. It took weeks to restore the harmony. This diner is a sanctuary, not a battlefield."

I exchanged a worried glance with Akira and Talia. "Do you know where she might be now?"

"I'm not sure, she always used to go to the Electric Gamebox arcade after eating here."

We all nodded and started heading towards the door.

"And you tell that lady, that I say she can take her attitude and shove it right up her-"

We left before she could finish.

"An arcade?" Akira said, raising an eyebrow. "What's Nemesis doing in an arcade? Playing Whack a Mortal?"

We exchanged uneasy glances as we left Demeter's Diner and made our way through the forest to the nearest train station. The night air was cool and filled with the sounds of rustling leaves and distant nocturnal animals. The anticipation of what lay ahead kept us moving swiftly, and soon we reached the small, dimly lit station.

We checked the times and the train to London was just pulling in, its headlights cutting through the darkness like beacons.

We boarded the train and found an empty compartment where we could sit together. The train's interior was warm and inviting, with plush seats and soft lighting that created a cosy atmosphere. As we settled in, the rhythmic clatter of the tracks began to soothe my nerves, and I glanced at Akira and Talia, feeling a sense of companionship and shared purpose.

Just as the train began to move, the compartment door slid open, and a girl with reddish-pinkish hair stepped in. She looked a few years older than us, yet she carried herself with confidence. Her emerald eyes darted around the compartment with a disdainful expression before her eyes landed on us. With an air of superiority, she strode over and took a seat opposite us, crossing her arms and glaring as if daring us to challenge her presence.

"What's your name?" Akira asked, her tone friendly and sweet.

"I'm Lady Gwen," she replied haughtily, flipping her vibrant hair over her shoulder, "and I don't appreciate sharing a compartment with... strangers."

"Well, it's a public train," I shot back, "you'll have to deal with it."

Lady Gwen rolled her eyes and muttered something under her breath. The tension in the compartment was awkward, but I tried to focus on the task at hand. We needed to get to London, find Nemesis, and uncover the truth behind the chaos that seemed to follow her.

As the train sped through the night, the scenery outside the window became a blur of dark fields and occasional lights from distant houses. The steady motion and the low hum of the train were almost hypnotic, but Lady Gwen's presence was like a thorn in our side. Her constant sighs and eye rolls grated on my nerves, but I reminded myself to stay focused.

"So, what brings you to London?" Lady Gwen finally asked, her tone dripping with sarcasm.

"We're on a mission," I replied curtly, not wanting to give away too much information.

Lady Gwen raised an eyebrow but didn't press further. Instead, she pulled out a sleek phone and began scrolling through it, occasionally glancing up at us with a look of disgust. Despite the uncomfortable atmosphere, we tried to relax and prepare for the challenges ahead. The train was our temporary refuge, and soon we would be thrown back into the heart of the mystery that awaited us in London.

The journey passed slowly, each minute feeling like an eternity under Lady Gwen's gaze. But as we drew closer to the city, a renewed sense of determination filled me. We were a step closer, to finding Nemesis, to meeting our dad, to going home, wherever that may be. As the train raced through the night, the tension in our compartment gradually became more bearable. Lady Gwen remained absorbed in her phone, occasionally throwing us disdainful glances, but we were too focused on our mission to let her attitude bother us much. I took the opportunity to go over our plan again in my mind, thinking about the best way to approach Nemesis once we found her. The thought of what might happen if we failed flickered in my mind, but I quickly pushed it aside. We couldn't afford to think like that.

Talia leaned closer to me and whispered, "Do you think Demeter was telling the truth about Nemesis and the arcade?" Her voice was barely audible over the hum of the train, but there was a genuine concern in her eyes.

"I don't know," I replied softly, "but we don't have any other leads. We have to check out the arcade, even if it's a long shot."

Akira, who had been quietly observing the countryside pass by, nodded in agreement. There was a hint of firmness in her eyes, and I knew she was just as determined as I was to get to the bottom of this mystery.

As we neared London, the landscape outside the window began to change. The dark fields and sparse lights gave way to the bright glow of the city. Tall buildings loomed in the distance, their lights twinkling like stars against the night sky.

The train slowed down as it approached the station, and an announcement crackled over the speakers, signalling our imminent arrival.

"We're almost there," Akira said, her voice tinged with excitement and a hint of nervousness. "Let's make sure we stick together once we get off the train. The city can be pretty overwhelming at night."

We all agreed, gathering our belongings and preparing to disembark. Lady Gwen, who had been silent for the last part of the journey, finally looked up from her phone and watched us with a strange expression on her face that was hard to read, a mixture of irritation, disdain and curiosity.

"Have you guys never been to London?" she asked with amusement in her voice.

"No," Talia said, "I haven't, I'm not sure about them."

This made Lady Gwen look even more curious, when the train finally came to a stop, we hurriedly made our way onto the platform. The hustle and bustle of London at night were invigorating, and the energy of the city seemed to seep into our veins, giving us a renewed sense of purpose. We navigated through the throngs of people, keeping an eye out for any signs or landmarks that might lead us to the Electric Gamebox Arcade.

Despite the late hour, the city was alive with activity, and the streets were filled with people going about their nightly routines.

- Chapter 6 -

Arcade Fun

After a short walk, we found ourselves standing in front of the arcade. The neon lights flashed brightly, casting colourful reflections on the wet pavement. The entrance was crowded with people, and the sound of electronic games and laughter spilled out into the street. This was it, our next step in the journey.

We exchanged determined glances, took a deep breath, and pushed our way through the crowd of people, entering the vibrant chaos of the arcade. Inside, the atmosphere was electric, with flashing screens and the constant beeping of game machines creating an uproar of sound.

"Let's split up and look for her," Akira suggested, "keep your phones on and stay in touch."

We nodded in agreement and went our separate ways, weaving through the crowd as we searched for any sign of Nemesis, or I thought we were going separately until I realised that Talia was walking behind me, I decided not to try to talk to her, my heart pounded with anticipation, and I couldn't shake the feeling that we were on the brink of something significant.

The vibrant energy of the arcade was almost overwhelming, but I pushed forward, determined to find the elusive goddess and uncover the truth.

Suddenly, I noticed someone, the girl from the first train journey, Nyx! What was she doing here?

Talia seemed to have noticed too and was heading right towards her.

Nyx eyed Talia as if she was a worthless trinket, "Talia, nice to see you again," she said, her tone cold.

"Hang on one second-" I said jumping in "Nemesis is your daughter right? Why can't you just find her?"

Nyx sighed, "It's not that simple child, you see she left with no warning, she's only gone into the human realm three times before and I was with her. She's never used her mortal form, so I won't know what she looks like."

"Mortal form?" I asked.

Nyx's lips curled into a sly smile, her gaze piercing through me with extreme intensity. "Ah, mortal forms," she murmured as if relishing the opportunity to tell us forbidden knowledge.

"Yes, you see, Nemesis, like many of our kind, possess the ability to look like a mortal to walk amongst your kind without arousing suspicion. It is a gift and a curse," she spun around to show us that she was in her mortal form.

"So, how are we meant to find her? We have no money and no idea where she could be?"

"If I knew, she wouldn't still be out here, would she?"

Nyx's gaze lingered on Talia for a moment longer, a hint of curiosity in her eyes. I then handed her a stack of cash.

"If you need any resources to find her," she said, her tone still firm, "and Talia," she added, her voice softer but still edged with that cold detachment, "that permanent smile of yours, it's always been quite unsettling."

Talia's smile remained unchanged, but her eyes flashed with a mix of comfort and something I couldn't quite understand. "I love you too, Grandma," she replied, her tone even.

With that, we turned back to the task at hand, the urgency of our mission pulling us forward into the chaotic energy of the arcade. Maybe Nemesis was here, Nyx didn't know what she looked like and come to think of it neither did I. So I did the only logical thing and asked Talia, though I knew I would regret it.

"She's gorgeous, absolutely stunning, long black hair and the same eyes as mine and-" she paused. "But noone has ever seen her mortal form, so she'll look different."

"And? Anything else about her? Face shape? height?"

She looked at me and scrunched her face up, still with a smile obviously, "-I don't remember anything else."

I stared at her, how could you not know what your own mother looked like? I hadn't seen my mother since I was five years old, but I remembered exactly what she looked like, and

Talia hadn't seen her mother in what... a year?

"It's been a while," she laughed nervously.

"How long?"

Then Akira came running up to us, "Find anything?"

"No," then we told her what Nyx had told us.

"Me neither, maybe she's not here?" she panted.

Disappointed but not discouraged, we continued our search through the maze of flashing lights and ringing machines. Each step felt heavier as the minutes passed, the initial excitement of the arcade fading into frustration. I scanned the faces of the crowd, hoping to catch a glimpse of Nemesis among them, but it was like searching for a needle in a haystack.

The air was thick with the smell of popcorn and fried food, the noise of the arcade blending into a chaotic symphony that made it difficult to focus.

I checked my phone for any messages or calls, but there was nothing. I wasn't sure who would call, I wasn't exactly Mr Popular, but I thought maybe a mysterious hint would pop up about where to find her. It seemed like Nemesis was determined to remain hidden, and the odds were stacked against us, why had she left? Why didn't she tell her mum? Did she want to be found?

As I walked, I couldn't shake the feeling of being watched. Every shadow seemed to hold a secret, every corner hiding a potential clue. But no matter how hard I looked, there was nothing but the swirling chaos of the arcade around me.

I tried to push aside the growing sense of unease and concentrate on the task at hand. We had come too far to give up now, but with each passing moment, it felt like our chances of finding Nemesis were slipping away.

Minutes turned into hours as we combed through every inch of the arcade, our determination slowly giving way to exhaustion. The once vibrant atmosphere now felt suffocating, the neon lights blurring together into a dizzying kaleidoscope of colour.

Finally, defeated and deflated, we regrouped near the entrance of the arcade. Akira looked weary, her usually sharp eyes dulled by fatigue. "I don't think she's here," she said, her voice heavy with disappointment.

I nodded in agreement, my own disappointment weighing heavily on my shoulders. We had searched every corner, questioned everyone, but it seemed that Nemesis had vanished without a trace.

As we made our way back onto the rain-soaked streets, I couldn't help but feel a sense of defeat wash over me. The neon lights of the arcade flickered behind us, a constant reminder of our failed mission. But amidst the disappointment, there was still a glimmer of hope. We may not have found Nemesis tonight, but our journey was far from over. We needed to find Nemesis and had to.

We set up camp right there on the streets, we didn't bother to try and find a forest this time. Akira quickly went to set up the tent, down a hidden alley. Leaving Talia and I on our own.

"I'm uh- sorry, that we didn't find your mum," I offered.

"Thank you," she said, her voice barely above a whisper.

We sat in silence for a while, the hum of the city around us filling the void. I glanced at Talia, her expression unreadable as she stared off into the distance. It was hard to believe that behind that permanent smile lay a storm of emotions she rarely let show.

"Do you think we'll ever find her?" I asked, hoping to break through the wall she had put up.

Talia turned to me, her smile still in place but her eyes betraying a flicker of doubt. "I hope so, I really do."

I nodded but didn't know what else to do or say. After we made sure the tent was secure, the three of us huddled inside, the sounds of the city muffled by the thin fabric walls. The rain continued to fall outside, a steady rhythm that contrasted sharply with the chaos of the arcade. The small space felt cramped, filled with unspoken thoughts and lingering tension.

Akira broke the silence first. "So, what now? Do we have any leads or are we just going to wander aimlessly?" Her voice was edged with frustration, and I couldn't blame her. We had come so far, only to be met with another dead end.

I sighed, running a hand through my hair. "We need to think strategically. Nyx mentioned that

Nemesis had never used her mortal form before. Maybe we can find someone who has seen her transform or knows more about how these forms work."

"We can try, but my mother, she never really talked about any friends."

"So what? She had no friends?"

Talia nodded and sighed, "She came to visit a few times but every other time Nyx had to come get me and bring me to their house."

"Their house, why don't we just look there?"

"Nyx lives there, you don't think she would have looked?"

"Right, of course."

We all came up with ideas but no matter how good they were, they would have all failed.

We sat in the tent, the rain creating a steady drumming on the fabric above us. The city outside was alive with sounds, but inside our small shelter, the silence was heavy with frustration and doubt. Each of us was lost in our own thoughts, trying to piece together a plan from the fragments of information we had.

Akira, ever the strategist, broke the silence again. "What about allies? Does Nyx have any friends who might want to help us, or at least have some information?"

Talia sighed "Nyx is... complicated, she keeps herself to herself."

How could she remember her grandmother's attitude and actions but not remember how her own mum looked?

"Back to square one then," Akira said, "maybe we should just try and rest up for now. Reluctantly, we all agreed. The tent, though small and cramped, offered a temporary respite from the storm of confusion and frustration swirling around us.

As we settled in for the night, my mind raced with unanswered questions and potential strategies. Despite the exhaustion, sleep seemed a distant prospect, overshadowed by the daunting task that lay ahead.

As I lay I thought of scenarios, plans forming and dissolving in the haze of fatigue. Eventually, sleep took over, pulling me into a restless slumber.

In the dim light of early morning, I awoke to find the girls still asleep. Talia lay curled up in a corner of the tent. Her long hair splayed out like a dark halo, and for once, her smile wasn't fully absent but it was more... human, replaced by a soft, almost vulnerable expression. She looked so different sleeping even if she was smiling, so fragile as if the weight of her emotions had finally lifted, if only for a moment.

Akira, on the other hand, seemed restless even in her sleep. Her brows were furrowed, and she shifted frequently as if wrestling with dreams as challenging as the reality we faced. Her normally sharp features softened in sleep.

The morning light filtered through the tent, casting a soft glow on their faces. I took a moment to observe them, my companions on this strange and perilous journey. Despite the chaos and uncertainty, there was a bond forming between us, forged in the fires of our shared mission.

I quietly slipped out of the tent, careful not to wake them. The city was still waking up, the early morning mist hanging in the air. The streets were quieter now, a stark contrast to the vibrant chaos of the night before. I took a deep breath, trying to shake off the remnants of my troubled dreams.

As I stood there, the events of the previous night replayed in my mind. Nyx's cryptic words, Talia's fleeting memories of her mother, and the overwhelming task of finding Nemesis. It felt like we were chasing shadows, but giving up was not an option.

Returning to the tent, I found Akira stirring awake, her eyes opening slowly, still clouded with sleep.

"Morning," I whispered, not wanting to disturb Talia. She nodded in acknowledgment, rubbing her eyes as she sat up.

"Any new ideas?" she asked, her voice husky with sleep.

"Not yet," I admitted, "but I was thinking, maybe we should head to a library or find someone who knows more about gods and their mortal forms. There has to be some way to track Nemesis."

Akira nodded, a glimmer of hope in her eyes. "It's worth a shot. Let's wait for Talia to wake up, and then we can start our search."

- Chapter 7 -

Myths and Mr Maverick

When Talia finally awoke we packed up the tent and shoved in it Akira's rucksack and walked the three minutes towards the library, when we reached it it read, 'OPENS AT 10:00'.

I peeked inside to see a huge clock on the wall and it read 09:00, we would just have to wait. We sat on the steps of the library, the cool stone offering a brief respite from the hectic night before. The city was slowly coming to life, the streets filling with people on their morning routines. Talia was unusually quiet and was twiddling her fingers. Akira leaned against the wall, lost in her thoughts. I decided to go get some coffee for all of us from a nearby cafe.

As the minutes ticked by, I couldn't help but reflect on our journey so far. It had been a whirlwind of confusion and discovery, each step bringing us closer to answers but also more questions.

The thought of Nemesis, somewhere out there, kept me driven, even if the path was unclear.

I looked at the clock again '09:30'. It still wasn't time for the library to open, I scooted over to Akira and she put her arms around me, offering a small piece of comfort.

Akira's mossy eyes darted over to Talia, "Are you alright?"

She looked back at us, widening her smile and nodded, weirdo. The wait felt unbearable. Every few moments, I found myself glancing at the clock, willing the hands to move faster. The city's bustle seemed to amplify our impatience, each passerby a reminder of how time slowed down when anticipation loomed. We tried to distract ourselves with small talk and observations about the people and architecture around us, but the conversation kept drifting back to Nemesis and the mysteries we were so desperate to unravel. Talia's silence was pleasant, though unusual, her fingers tracing invisible patterns on the steps as if trying to write the answers that eluded us.

At one point, a street musician set up nearby and started playing a melancholic tune on his violin. The haunting notes filled the air, creating a soundtrack for our wait. It was as if the city itself was acknowledging our anxious feelings. The music intertwined with my thoughts, making the moment feel both timeless and fleeting. The contrast between the urgency of our quest and the slow, deliberate movements of the clock created a suspense that was almost unbearable.

Despite the uncertainty, Akira's arm around me provided a small anchor, a reminder that we were in this together and would always have each other no matter what, I knew we would always be together and I knew we would find Nemesis.

The minutes dragged on, each second stretching longer than the last. The sun climbed higher, casting shifting shadows on the steps where we sat. Occasionally, a passerby would glance at us with curiosity or sympathy, but we remained quiet, focused on the clock and the promise it held. We passed around a water bottle, the cool liquid offering a brief distraction from the oppressive wait. The anticipation was almost physical, a tightness in my chest that refused to loosen.

By 09:45, our restlessness was tangible. Talia had begun pacing in small circles, her fingers now tugging at the ends of her hair. Akira, usually so composed, tapped her foot in a rhythmic pattern that seemed to echo the ticking of the clock. I closed my eyes, trying to steady my breathing, to centre myself amidst the chaos of thoughts. The library stood tall and silent before us, a fortress of knowledge that seemed tantalisingly out of reach. Each tick of the clock was a reminder of how close we were, yet how interminable the wait felt.

Finally, as the clock inched towards 10 o'clock, a subtle shift occurred. The energy around us changed, a collective breath held in anticipation.

We gathered our belongings, standing up and stretching our muscles, stiff from sitting too long. The library doors, still closed, seemed to beckon us with silent promise. The moment we had been waiting for was almost here. Talia, Akira, and I exchanged a look of determination. Whatever lay beyond those doors, we would face it together, ready to uncover the secrets that awaited us inside.

A small wiry man started walking towards us shoving us out of the way to get to the big mahogany doors. He unlocked three large bolts and turned what seemed to be the largest key ever in the ornate lock and pushed open the door, walked inside and flipped the sign that said closed until 10 o'clock.

We ran into the library and started looking for books about mortal forms or Greek mythology but we couldn't find anything. We continued looking around for some but we didn't see any books to do with mythology, so we headed over to the man, who had a dark brown buzzcut and small eyes hiding behind his dirty spectacles.

"Hello, Sir?"

"What do you want?" he said in a hoarse voice, that sounded as if he had gunk built up in his throat from the past eight years.

"Do you have any books on Greek mythology?"

He snorted and started having coughing spasms.

"Sir?"

"Mr Maverick," he managed to splutter out.

"Alright then... Mr Maverick, was that a yes?"

"Mythology?" he said slowly in a quiet raspy voice and then it started getting higher until he began shouting.

"THAT THING IS A LOAD OF NONSENSE!"

Talia covered her ears with her ghostly pale skin.

"WHY WOULD WE STOCK UP THE LIBRARY WITH SUCH NONSENSE?!"

I locked eyes with him and pointed at the 'no loud-speaking' sign, which only made him angrier and louder. I honestly thought my cheek would meet the back of his hand, so I stepped back. Akira stepped forward and put on her most soothing voice that she always used to use for me when I couldn't sleep. "We respect your opinion, but we need to find somewhere that does, do you know anywhere that has some?"

"No and even if I did, why would I tell you?"

Mr. Maverick's tirade had escalated quickly, his voice reverberating off the library walls like thunder. Talia, still smiling but visibly uncomfortable, looked on with wide eyes, her hands clutched her ears so tightly you could see some pink peaking through. Akira's calm demeanour was a stark contrast to Mr. Maverick's outburst, her voice a soothing balm amidst the chaos.

With a flick of my wrist, I brushed off some nonexistent dust from my shirt and stepped forward, meeting Mr. Maverick's fiery gaze with an arched eyebrow.

"Well, Mr. Maverick, it seems you've mistaken this library for your own personal soapbox. While we appreciate your vocal enthusiasm, we're not here for a debate on your literary preferences. We're simply seeking information, which, if you could muster the decency, you might assist us with."

Mr. Maverick's face flushed with indignation, his fists clenching at his sides. "You insolent little -" he began, but I cut him off with a wave of my hand.

"Save your breath, Mr. Maverick, your volume far exceeds your threatening tone," I retorted with a confidence I wasn't sure I had, earning a surprised chuckle from Akira.

She stepped in smoothly, her voice still as serene as ever. "Now, if you could kindly direct us to a more accommodating establishment, we'll be on our way. We wouldn't want to disturb the peace of your precious library any further."

Mr Maverick still didn't tell us so we turned to leave, deciding it was futile to reason with him any longer. As we walked away from the library, I couldn't shake off the feeling of frustration mingled with disappointment. It seemed our quest for knowledge hit a dead end, at least for the moment. Every turn we made seemed to lead to nowhere and I could tell the feeling of hopelessness was thought but not said.

Talia's shoulders sagged a bit, her earlier energy dampened by the encounter with Mr. Maverick. Akira walked beside me, her expression thoughtful. "Well," she said after a moment, "it looks like we'll have to find another source for information on Greek mythology."

Akira took out her phone from her jeans pocket and looked up libraries near us, "This is the only library near us unless we go back to HollowHead High," we looked at each other and I shuddered, it would be a little weird to go back to school a few days after leaving then returning not to long after without our 'uncle'.

"Do they have Greek books there?" Talia asked, her ears getting less pinker by the second.

"Yeah, but I don't know if we are still enrolled in school or not," Akira told her, "I don't think Hermes would withdraw us from school if we are able to go back but I'm not sure."

"He doesn't normally, Cyanide and Shanda Anschutz arrived at camp last year from a school in Germany, they stayed for a while then left to go back to their original school."

I looked at Akira and she looked at me with a glimmer of determination in her mossy eyes. "Well, I suppose it's worth a shot. If we can't find what we need at this library, then HollowHead High might be our next best option."

I glanced at Talia, who seemed to be regaining her composure, her fingers no longer fidgeting nervously.

"And if we're not enrolled anymore, we'll figure something out, we always do," Akira continued.

With a renewed sense of purpose, we set off towards HollowHead High, the prospect of revisiting our old school bringing a mix of nostalgia and apprehension. As we walked, I couldn't help but feel nervous.

As we approached the familiar gates of HollowHead High, memories flooded back, both pleasant and painful, actually nothing pleasant, for me at least. The towering brick walls seemed to whisper secrets of the past, reminding us of the battles we fought and the friendships we forged within its halls, maybe not ours but friendships nonetheless. But now, returning under different circumstances, I felt even worse than I would have if we came back if we wanted to resume the year.

We pushed open the big metal gates, walked inside and headed straight to Miss Olivia's office. We walked down the familiar corridors of HollowHead High, the echoes of our footsteps reverberating against the cold, unforgiving walls. As we reached Miss Olivia's office, a knot formed in my stomach, with the feeling of nausea.

Talia reached out and knocked on the door, the sound echoing in the silence of the hallway. After a moment, the door creaked open, revealing Miss Olivia sitting behind her desk, her expression unreadable. She regarded us with a cool detachment, her eyes flickering over each of us in turn.

"Good morning, Miss Olivia," Akira greeted her, her voice steady despite the tension in the room, "we were hoping to speak with you."

Miss Olivia arched an eyebrow, her gaze lingering on each of us in turn. "And what brings you here today and where's your uncle? Is everything okay?" she asked, her voice as crisp as the morning air.

"Yes, he's, uhh- at home. We're looking for information on Greek mythology," I said, meeting her gaze head-on. "We were wondering if the school library might have some resources that could help us if we still have access to it."

Miss Olivia's lips curved into a small, wry smile. "Greek mythology, is it?" she mused, tapping her fingers thoughtfully against her desk. "An interesting choice of study, I'm sure we have books on that and yes you still have access to the library, you're still enrolled in school."

I nodded. Miss Olivia had always been a mystery to us, her demeanour distant yet not unkind. It was hard to tell what she was thinking, what secrets lay hidden behind those cool, calculating eyes. She was kind to everyone yet didn't seem to have favourites, most of the time.

"And who is this?" she asked suddenly, her gaze settling on Talia. "I don't believe we've had the pleasure of meeting."

Talia stood beside us, her smile as bright and permanent as ever. "This is Talia," Akira replied smoothly, stepping forward to stand beside her. "She's... a friend of ours."

Miss Olivia's eyes narrowed slightly, a flicker of judgement dancing in their depths. She regarded Talia with a silent judgement, her lips pressed into a thin line. It was clear that she was forming her own opinions about Talia, though she kept them carefully concealed beneath her composed exterior.

"I see," she said quietly, though there was a hint of scepticism in her voice, "well, it's a pleasure to meet you, Talia."

Talia offered a wider smile in return, her fingers twisting nervously in the fabric of her shirt. Miss Olivia's silent judgement hung in the air between us, a subtle reminder of the barriers that existed within the walls of HollowHead High.

- Chapter 8 -

Reuniting with Demi Jones

As we were walking towards the school library, the familiar, albeit unpleasant, chatter of students reached our ears. The whispers and glances reminded us that we were not exactly returning to friendly territory. HollowHead High was a battleground of cliques and power plays, and we were stepping right back into the fray.

Suddenly, a loud, mocking voice echoed down the hallway. "Well, well, well, look who decided to show their faces again!" Demi Jones sauntered toward us, her posse, including Brooklyn Johansen, trailing behind like shadows. Demi's eyes gleamed with malicious delight, clearly relishing this unexpected confrontation.

"What do you want, Demi?" I asked, trying to keep my voice steady. Akira tensed beside me, her jaw set in a hard line.

Demi laughed, a harsh, grating sound. "Just catching up with old friends, Oliver. Oh, and who's this?" She turned her gaze to Talia, her lips curling into a smirk. "Is this your girlfriend?"

'So gross!' I thought, although I didn't give her the satisfaction of a reply.

"What's wrong with her eyes, are they some type of freaky contacts?" she snarled pointing at Talia's pitch-black eyes

Talia's smile widened for a moment, her black eyes with streaks of gold shimmering under the harsh fluorescent lights. She remained silent, but I could see her fingers twitching at her sides, the only sign of her discomfort.

"Leave her alone, Demi," Akira said, stepping forward. Her mossy eyes flashed with anger. "We're not here for your games."

"Oh, but I think you are," Brooklyn chimed in, her voice dripping with scornfulness.

"It's so cute how you always play the protector, Akira. How's that working out for you?"

Demi's eyes flicked back to me. "And you, Oliver. Still chasing after myths and legends? Found any monsters yet?"

The taunts hit harder than I cared to admit, especially since we had. The cruel, mocking tone brought back memories of every sneer and snide remark we'd endured at HollowHead High. But I refused to give Demi the satisfaction of seeing us break.

"Let's just go," I muttered to Akira and Talia, turning away from the sneering faces.

But Demi wasn't done. She reached out and shoved Akira, causing her to stumble. "Don't turn your back on me," Demi hissed, "I'm not finished."

Akira regained her balance and squared her shoulders, facing Demi with a steely determination. "Yes, you are, we're done here."

Brooklyn laughed, stepping closer to me. "You know," she eyed Talia, "you should really rethink those contacts. It's like you're trying to be some kind of freak. Oh wait, you already are."

Talia's smile wavered, but she kept her composure. "Thanks for the advice, but I think I'll pass."

Demi moved closer, her face inches from Akira's. "You think you're so brave, don't you? Always playing the hero. But heroes fall, Akira, they always fall."

I clenched my fists, stepping forward to put myself between Demi and Akira. "Back off, Demi, we're not here to fight."

"Oh, I know," Demi said, her voice sickeningly sweet, "but where's the fun in that? You see, Oliver, people like you and Akira are just so easy to rile up, and you," she added, casting a disdainful glance at Talia, "you're just the perfect little weirdo to complete the trio."

Brooklyn nudged Demi with a smirk. "I bet Oliver likes that, though. Guys always go for the strange ones, don't they, Oliver?"

My anger flared, but I forced myself to stay calm, she wasn't my friend, we had been thrown together in this quest, so she definitely wasn't my girlfriend. "Come on, let's go. They're not worth our time."

As we turned to leave, Demi's parting shot hit harder than any physical blow. "Good luck finding those Greek myths, losers, yes we overheard what you're looking for. Maybe you'll find a nice fairy tale to live in."

We walked away, our backs straight, but the sting of their words lingered. Once we were out of earshot, Akira exhaled sharply, her hands trembling. "They're worse than ever."

Talia's earlier silence finally broke. "I don't get why they're so mean. Do they really enjoy hurting others?"

"Yes," Akira said softly, "they do."

We continued to the library in silence, the encounter with Demi and Brooklyn casting a dark cloud over our mood. The familiar corridors, once a place of dread, now seemed even more oppressive. But we pushed forward, determined to find what we came for.

Inside the library, the musty smell of old books greeted us. The rows of shelves were filled with countless volumes, a labyrinth of knowledge. We split up, each of us scanning the shelves for anything related to Greek mythology.

After what felt like hours, Akira called out softly, "I found something."

We gathered around her, looking at the book she held. It was old, its leather cover worn and faded. The title, "Mythos: Legends of Ancient Greece," was embossed in gold lettering.

"This might be what we need," Akira said, a note of hope in her voice, "let's see what we can find."

We settled at a table in the back corner of the library, the book open between us. As we pored over its pages, the weight of the morning's events began to lift. The knowledge contained within these ancient myths offered a glimmer of hope, a chance to find the answers we so desperately sought.

And as we read, the library's quiet sanctuary shielded us from the outside world, if only for a little while. We were together, and in this moment, that was enough.

Sitting at the table, the ancient book titled, "Mythos: Legends of Ancient Greece," lay open before us. The quiet rustle of pages and the faint scent of old leather gave me a warm and relaxed feeling, a momentary refuge from the harsh reality outside and what could be awaiting us.

"Look at this," Akira said, pointing to a passage that seemed promising. "This chapter talks about the mortal forms of gods. It might have something useful."

We leaned in, our heads nearly touching as we scanned the text. The book was filled with elaborate illustrations and detailed stories of gods and heroes, but the more we read, the clearer it became that this was a work of fiction, not a factual account.

"This can't be right," I muttered, flipping through the pages in frustration, "these are just stories, myths. There's nothing here that can help us."

Akira's shoulders slumped, "So, it's just a fairy tale book," Akira said quietly, "everything we've been through, all the clues...for nothing."

I closed the book with a sigh, the sense of defeat weighing heavily on us. "Let's just get out of here," I said, "we'll find another way."

As we left the library, the disappointment was discernible. The sun had dipped lower in the sky, casting long shadows across the school grounds. We walked in silence, each of us lost in our thoughts.

Suddenly, a voice cut through the quiet. "Well, look who it is," Demi sneered, stepping out from behind a tree with Brooklyn by her side. They had been waiting for us.

"Did you find your little fairy tales?" Brooklyn mocked, her eyes gleaming with malice.

"Leave us alone, Demi," Akira said, her voice weary, "we're not in the mood."

Demi's smile turned sinister. "Oh, but we are." She stepped forward and without warning, shoved me hard against the wall. Pain shot through my shoulder as I collided with the rough brick surface. I wanted to fight back, I wasn't weak but fighting with girls even if they were being mean just didn't sit right with me.

Akira moved to help me, but Brooklyn grabbed her arm and twisted it painfully behind her back. "You really should learn when to quit," Brooklyn hissed.

"Stop it!" Talia shouted, but Demi only laughed.

"Or what?" Demi taunted. "What are you going to do about it, weirdo?"

I struggled to push Demi away, but she was relentless, her fists striking with brutal precision. Akira cried out in pain as Brooklyn's grip tightened, forcing her to her knees.

"Why do you always do this?" I managed to gasp, trying to shield myself from Demi's blows.

"Because it's fun," Demi said coldly, delivering a final kick to my ribs before stepping back.

Brooklyn released Akira, who fell to the ground, clutching her arm. "Remember this the next time you think about coming back here," Brooklyn spat.

They walked away, laughing and high-fiving each other, leaving us battered and bruised on the ground. Talia rushed to help Akira up, her hands trembling.

"Are you okay?" Talia asked, her voice shaking.

Akira winced, holding her arm. "I'll be fine, let's just get out of here."

We helped each other up, moving slowly and painfully away from the school. The encounter had left us shaken, our bodies aching from the assault, but our resolve remained unbroken.

"We can't let them win," I said through gritted teeth, the pain in my ribs making it hard to speak.

"Why don't you just, you know.... fight back," Talia said.

"I thought you didn't like revenge," I managed to wheeze through the pain.

"I said, we define our own paths, not inheriting our parents' identities unless we decide to, you may choose to get revenge, I can't decide for you. Just because I don't resort to something right away, doesn't mean it's the wrong choice for you." Talia's words hung in the air, a reminder of the different perspectives we brought to the table.

Akira sighed heavily, her gaze fixed on the ground as we walked. "It's not that simple, Talia. Fighting back only fuels their fire. We've been down that road before."

"But what else can we do?" I asked, frustration lacing my voice. "We can't just let them walk all over us. I"m fed up with not retaliating, they are getting worse and worse."

Talia's expression softened, her eyes reflecting understanding. "Maybe there's another way to fight back, one that doesn't involve stooping to their level."

Akira glanced up, curiosity piqued. "What do you mean?"

"I mean we hit them where it hurts the most," Talia said, a hint of determination in her voice, "their reputation."

I furrowed my brow, trying to follow her line of thinking. "How?"

"We expose them," Talia explained, "we gather evidence of their bullying, their cruelty, and we bring it to light."

Akira's eyes widened with realisation. "You mean like a... a campaign?"

"Exactly," Talia nodded, "we make it known to everyone what kind of people they really are. We really support, empower those who've been silent victims, and together, we stand against them."

A glimmer of hope sparked within me, igniting a newfound resolve. "It's risky," I admitted, "but it might be our best shot."

"We can't let them keep getting away with this," Akira agreed, determination firming her jaw.

Talia smiled, a small but genuine expression of optimism. "Then it's settled, we fight back, but on our own terms."

As we made our way through the halls of HollowHead High, we couldn't ignore the sidelong glances and whispered taunts that followed us like shadows. Demi and Brooklyn's popularity cast a long shadow, and many students seemed eager to align themselves with them, hoping to bask in the reflected glow of their social status.

Among those who joined in the mockery were Drew Henderson, a smooth-talking charmer whose wit cut sharper than any blade, and Nilo Adzerbask, whose quick temper and biting sarcasm made him a formidable foe.

Lily Laughton, with her clique of followers trailing behind her like obedient puppies, took every opportunity to belittle us, her laughter ringing in our ears like a constant reminder of our outsider status.

And then there was Diego Garcia, the epitome of the entitled jock stereotype. With his towering frame and arrogant swagger, he ruled the school with an iron fist, his loyal band of football cronies trailing behind him like obedient lackeys. Diego took pleasure in targeting anyone he deemed beneath him, his cruelty matched only by his wealth and influence.

Their laughter echoed in the hallways, a chorus of disdain that seemed to follow us wherever we went. But despite their best efforts to break our spirits, we remained steadfast, refusing to bow to their tyranny.

As we returned to the library, the air crackled with tension, our footsteps echoing in the silent corridor. But just as we reached the entrance, a familiar voice cut through the quiet like a knife.

"Well, well, well, what do we have here?" Diego Garcia leaned against the wall, his grin as smug as ever. His football cronies flanked him, their presence looming like an ominous shadow.

"What's this I hear about a little campaign against Demi and Brooklyn?" Diego drawled, his tone dripping with condescension. "You guys really think you stand a chance against us?"

Akira squared her shoulders, her gaze steady. "We're not afraid of you, Diego and we won't back down."

Diego's laughter filled the hallway, a booming sound that sent shivers down our spines. "Oh, I love it when you talk tough, Akira. It's almost cute."

He sauntered forward, his eyes lingering on Talia, who stood beside me with a puzzled expression. Talia, unlike the others, had always seemed oblivious to social cues, especially when it came to matters of affection or flirtation.

"So, what's your role in all of this, sweetheart?" Diego asked, his voice laced with false sweetness. "Are you the brains behind the operation?"

Talia furrowed her brow, confusion evident in her expression. "I don't understand," she said simply, her tone devoid of any flirtatious undertones.

Diego's smile faltered for a moment, taken aback by Talia's lack of response. He cleared his throat, trying to regain his composure. "Uh, I mean, are you part of the group too?"

"Yes," Talia replied matter-of-factly, her focus returning to the task at hand.

As Diego turned his attention back to Akira, his football teammates, Xavier Mount, Gregor Nead, and Danny Brock, stepped forward, attempting their own flirtations. Xavier, with his charming smile and confident demeanour, tried to engage Akira in witty banter. Gregor, with his shy but earnest attempts at conversation, focused his attention on Talia, complimenting her intelligence and unique perspective. Danny, the class clown of the group, cracked jokes and made playful remarks in an attempt to win over both Akira and Talia.

But Talia, oblivious to their advances, remained focused on our mission, her attention unwavering. She didn't seem to understand flirty or affection in general.

As we entered the library, the awkward attempts at distraction lingered in the air, a reminder of the challenges we faced both inside and outside its walls. But we refused to let their antics derail us from our mission. For we were united in our cause, determined to stand up against injustice no matter the cost. And for Talia, it was just another reminder of her struggle to comprehend the complexities of human interaction. I couldn't help but feel a pang of empathy for Talia.

Despite our differences, it didn't sit right to see her subjected to the shallow advances of Diego's football teammates. I wasn't sure about Talia, not even as a friend, but I didn't want to see her get played, it wasn't right. They had tried to convince Akira to date them but she refused because Akira has standards.

As we headed round the corner we bumped into a woman, with flaming red hair, Mrs Scythe.

"I thought I recognised those faces," she smiled warmly at us, "what are you doing back?"

"Just looking for something," Akira smiled back.

"What is it, I could help if you wanted."

"A book, Greek mythology, mortal forms?" I wasn't sure how much information was too much, we needed enough so she knew what we needed but not too much that she would get suspicious.

Whilst Mrs Scythe went to see what she could find, we tried to act normal, which was hard with Talia running around with a lack of human understanding, and somehow a lack of school etiquette, if it was almost as if she had never gone to a proper school before. People looked at her weirdly whenever they passed her in the hallway. Even teachers looked at her oddly, except Mrs Scythe who after bringing us a book, that didn't sound completely fake, had tested out all of our Greek, making sure we were catching up on our lessons, and decided to check Talia's too, for fun maybe, or perhaps she was just being a teacher. She actually seemed quite intrigued by Talia, especially by her eyes and smile and was over the moon when she heard Talia's Greek. I was pretty sure she was fluent, but she still didn't know a few words in English, which was quite surprising. Mostly words to do with affection. Whilst the two of them chatted in Greek, Akira and I studied the book and took a photo with Akira's phone, so we could look back whenever we needed to. The sources seemed true enough.

"Thank you so much Mrs Scythe, you have no idea how much you just helped us," I said, handing her the book back.

She just handed it back to me and winked, "I think I have an idea."

I didn't really know what she meant by that but I decided not to dwell on it. I stuffed the book in my bag and smiled politely.

"I wish we could stay, to put Demi and Brooklyn in their place," Akira sighed, "but we should probably get going and just maybe there will be an opportunity in the future, who knows."

- Chapter 9 -

The Quest Continues

In all the chaos unfolding at school, I realised we had got distracted from our goal in finding Nemesis, how Nyx must be feeling, how Talia must be feeling. I felt bad, though I would never admit it. I realised we had gotten preoccupied with trying to find the book, instead of taking proper action.

We left really late that evening and packed Akira's small bag filled with both of our few belongings and the tent. We headed towards the iron gates and left, not bothering to tell anyone or write a note.

"So where are we going now?" I asked, "Anywhere else your mother likes to go?"

"I don't think so."

"Great! Just great," I muttered under my breath but Akira must have heard and given me a look, half empathy and half, shut up she's doing the best she can.

"Where is a place a goddess would hang out?"

"She is the Goddess of revenge, what about a courthouse or something."

Talia gave us a quizzical look, "A Goddess might hang out at a temple, a shrine."

"Do they have temples to Greek gods in England?" Akira asked.

"I don't think so, they're Greek we are not in Greece."

"Maybe we should try Nyx's house, if I was to run away I would keep moving, not stay in one place. You got to be on the move, so no one finds you."

"You're right, Nemesis probably didn't stay in one place for all this time."

"Their house is probably hidden, right Talia?" I asked, I still didn't trust her but she was our best hope, she didn't give us a reason not to trust her, except for that smile, I just had a hunch.

"It's in a forest somewhere, a cave I think."

"Great," I muttered, a heavy dose of sarcasm lacing my voice, "because there are only a thousand forests in England."

"I know its in London, so that takes out quite a few."

"Yeah, great!"

Akira shot me a glare, and I could see the frustration in her eyes. "We don't have a choice, Oliver, we have to try."

We spent the next few days trudging through various forests, each one looking more like a scene from a fairy tale than the last. We followed Talia's vague memories of her mother's cave, but each time we thought we were getting close, the path would veer off into dense underbrush or lead us to a dead end.

"Lovely, another dead end," I sighed, kicking at a rock, "at this rate, we'll be senior citizens before we find anything."

"We have to keep looking," Akira said and I could hear the panic in her voice, was it because she really wanted to go back to camp? Or did she really want to finally meet our father?

"Don't worry, we will and we won't stop until we find her," I tried to comfort her and if I'm being honest, I needed it too. I was dirty, I was tired and I was starving. In the last few days, we ate most of our beef jerky and only had one packet left and we didn't know when we would find Nemesis, so we decided to save it to the best of our abilities.

"Let's go look somewhere else, there's a lot of forests, we can't be far." I grabbed her hand and squeezed it tight.

"What about this one?" I said reading the sign "Epping Forest."

"We can try," Akira said, looking at Talia. Who looked the same as always, smiling. That smile was seriously freaking me out, considering that there wasn't much to smile about at that moment.

As we entered Epping Forest, the dense canopy of trees provided a welcome shade from the relentless sun. The air was cool and crisp, carrying the earthy scent of pine and damp leaves. The sounds of birds chirping and the evergreen trees swayed in the breeze making sounds that resembled gentle whispers, creating an almost supernatural feel to our surroundings as we ventured deeper into the woods.

"This place is huge," I muttered, gazing around at the sprawling forest, "how are we supposed to find one cave in all of this, with no map?"

"We just have to keep looking," Akira replied, determination etched on her face, "we've come this far. We can't give up now."

Talia walked slightly ahead, her dark eyes scanning the surroundings. Despite my misgivings about her, I had to admit she had an amazing ability to navigate the forest. She seemed to know where to go, even if it was just a vague sense of direction.

As we walked, the forest grew denser, the trees standing like silent statues. The path we followed became less defined, narrowing to a barely visible trail covered in fallen pine cones and twigs. We stepped carefully, the crunching sound of our footsteps breaking the stillness.

"I hate to say it, but we might be lost," I said after a while, my voice tinged with frustration. "We've been walking for hours, and there's no sign of any cave."

Akira wiped the sweat from her brow and nodded. "I know it seems hopeless, but we can't turn back now. Talia, are you sure we're on the right track?"

Talia paused, her brow furrowing in concentration. "I'm not sure," she admitted, her voice soft, "it's been so long since I've been here, and the forest changes over time. But I feel like we're close."

I sighed, trying to push down the rising tide of irritation. "Feeling close isn't exactly reassuring when we've been wandering for hours."

Akira shot me a look, her eyes pleading for patience. "Let's keep going a bit longer. We can't give up just yet."

Reluctantly, I nodded, and we continued our trek through the woods. The forest seemed to close in around us, the trees growing thicker and the underbrush more tangled. Every now and then, we would stop to catch our breath, taking sips from our dwindling water supply.

The sun was beginning to dip lower in the sky, casting long shadows across the forest floor. The golden light filtered through the leaves, creating a dappled pattern on the ground. Despite the beauty of the scene, a sense of urgency gnawed at me. We couldn't afford to be out here after dark. We would need to make camp and trying to pitch the tent in the dark seemed near impossible.

"Look," Akira said suddenly, pointing to a clearing up ahead, "maybe there's something there."

We pushed through the dense foliage, emerging into a small clearing. The sunlight poured in, illuminating the space with a warm, golden glow of the evening sun. In the centre of the clearing stood a large, ancient oak tree, its gnarled branches reaching towards the sky.

"Well, it's not a cave," I said, trying to keep the disappointment out of my voice.

"But it's beautiful," Akira said softly, walking towards the tree. She placed a hand on its rough bark, a look of wonder on her face. "It's like something out of a fairy tale."

Talia joined her, her smile unwavering. "This tree is special, I can feel it. Even if we don't find the cave, being here is important."

I couldn't share their sense of awe. All I saw was another dead end, another failure. But I kept my thoughts to myself, not wanting to dampen their spirits.

As we rested in the clearing, the peacefulness of the place began to seep into me. I leaned against the trunk of the old oak tree, closing my eyes for a moment. The sounds of the forest seemed to lull me into a sense of calm, and for the first time in days, I felt a flicker of hope.

"Maybe we're not meant to find the cave right now," Akira said quietly, breaking the silence. "Maybe this is just a part of our journey, and we need to trust that we'll find our way when the time is right."

I opened my eyes and looked at her, seeing the determination and faith in her gaze. Despite everything, she still believed we could find Nemesis. And in that moment, I realised that belief was enough to keep me going.

"You're right," I said, pushing myself away from the tree, "we'll find her. Maybe not today, but we will and until then, we'll keep searching."

"We should probably get some rest," Akira said, busying herself with erecting the tent, "if we are going to find the cave tomorrow."

I woke up to a loud high-pitched scream, I knew it too well, so I rushed over to Akira who looked terrified.

"Are you ok? What happened?"

She gagged, "Something slimy and round touched my leg."

"It's probably just a frog," Talia tried to say soothingly.

But that made Akira scream louder, Akira had been terrified of frogs, ever since she was nine, why? I never knew.

Talia covered her ears, looked at the ground and started feeling around. "There's nothing here, it must have left."

Akira's breathing slowed down and the colour returned to her cheeks.

I went to grab some water from her backpack and suddenly tripped over something small and spherical.

"Oliver, are you ok?"

"Yeah," I said, trying to look around for the thing that had tripped me.

Was it a rock? Surely not, no rock would not be that round. Was it the frog? No, it didn't make a sound when I fell over it.

I felt around and suddenly touched something really sticky, I picked it up but I couldn't identify what it was, it was way too dark to see.

"Hey child," said a croaky voice, "can you pass me my eye."

I dropped the slimy object instantly.

"Our eye," repeated two more voices.

I ran away from the eye and wiped my hands on my t-shirt, yuk so gross.

"Uhhh, your eye?" Akira said nervously.

"Graeae, three old women, one eye and one tooth between them," Talia explained, eyeing them, though they were looking at where I was previously standing.

I looked at Talia with a look that said, who?

"Deino, Enyo, and Pemphredo-"

"Whilst we would love to make introductions, we need our eye back," she reached out her pasty, bony hand, to obviously touch my shoulder.

"Uhh, over here," I said, and she started walking the opposite way. "No, the other way."

I looked at her whilst she was walking towards me, she looked hideous, though I didn't dare say that aloud, she had a hunched-over posture and her empty eye sockets were haunting.

She took slow and steady steps towards me and finally reached out and touched my shoulder, her hand was dry and bony, her veins sticking out.

"Your eye is on the floor back there," I said, waiting for her to remove her hand. I wanted to tell her to take her hand off me but she seemed so old and I didn't want to be rude to an old woman.

Deino, Enyo, and Pemphredo turned as one and shuffled back towards the spot where I had dropped the eye. I felt a shiver run down my spine as I watched their gnarled hands patting the ground in search of the slimy orb. Talia stepped closer to me, her permanent smile unsettling in the dim light of the forest.

"We have to get out of here," Akira whispered urgently, "they're probably dangerous."

"No kidding," I muttered, glancing at Talia, "any bright ideas?"

Talia's smile widened. "We can't let them get their eye back. If they can't see, they can't follow us."

I looked over at the backpack and the sword lying next to it, if only I could get close enough.

As if on cue, the Graeae found the eye. Deino triumphantly held it aloft before placing it in her empty socket, which honestly made me want to throw up. The three hags turned to face us, their single eye gleaming in the moonlight.

"You've made a grave mistake, children," Enyo hissed, "no one escapes the Graeae."

Before we could react, the Graeae lunged at us with surprising speed. Despite their ancient appearance, they moved with the agility of predators, their bony fingers reaching out to grab us. I barely managed to dodge Deino's grasp, but Akira wasn't so lucky. Enyo had her in a vice-like grip, pulling her away from me.

"Let her go!" I shouted, fumbling for something, anything, to use as a weapon.

My hand closed around a thick branch, and I swung it wildly at Enyo. The branch connected with a sickening thud, and Enyo stumbled back, releasing Akira.

Talia jumped in, her movements fluid and precise. She grabbed another branch and began fending off the other two Graeae, who had turned their attention to her. Despite her smaller size, Talia's confidence and skill were evident. She moved with a grace that made it clear she knew what she was doing.

"Akira, run!" I yelled, but she hesitated, her eyes wide with fear and uncertainty.

"We have to fight them," Talia said, her voice calm and steady despite the chaos, "they won't stop until we're dead."

Akira nodded, her face pale but determined. She picked up a rock and stood beside me. "I'm not leaving you."

The Graeae regrouped, their single eye blazing with fury. "You think you can defeat us?" Pemphredo sneered. "We've lived for centuries. We are unbeatable."

Talia's smile didn't waver. "We'll see about that."

The fight began in earnest. Talia took the lead, her branch swinging in controlled arcs, keeping the Graeae at bay. Akira and I tried to mimic her movements, but it was clear we were out of our depth. The Graeae were relentless, their attacks precise and coordinated despite having only one eye.

Deino lunged at me, her fingers like claws. I swung my branch, but she dodged easily, her hand closing around my arm. I yelped in pain as her grip tightened, but before she could do more, Talia was there, knocking her back with a powerful strike. It looked like something fell to the ground but in the confusion, I couldn't see what it was, possibly just a bit of branch that had snapped off.

"Keep moving!" Talia instructed. "Don't let them corner you."

We followed her lead, darting around the clearing, trying to avoid the Graeae's attacks. Akira managed to land a hit on Pemphredo, who snarled in pain but didn't slow down. It was like fighting shadows; they were always one step ahead, always just out of reach.

In the chaos, I noticed something glinting in the moonlight. It was the Graeae's eye, it hadn't been a branch snapping, Talia had knocked it out when she hit Deino, it was lying on the ground where it had rolled during the fight. An idea formed in my mind, reckless and desperate.

"Talia, the eye!" I shouted, pointing.

She saw it and nodded. "Cover me."

I grabbed a handful of rocks and started throwing them at the Graeae, aiming to distract them. Akira followed suit, and for a moment, the three ancient sisters faltered, their attention divided. It was enough for Talia to make her move. She sprinted towards the eye, diving to the ground and grabbing it.

"Got it!" she yelled, holding the eye up high.

The Graeae screamed in rage, their voices a chorus of fury and desperation. "Give it back!" they shrieked, advancing on Talia.

"No way!" Talia said, her smile turning fierce. "You want it? Come and get it."

She threw the eye to me, and I caught it, feeling the slimy, squishy texture in my hand. Without thinking, I threw it to Akira, who tossed it back to Talia. The Graeae tried to follow, but we were faster, keeping the eye out of their reach.

The game of keep-away infuriated them, and they became more reckless in their attacks. Deino made a wild lunge at Akira, who barely dodged in time, stumbling over a root. I swung my branch at Enyo, but she caught it, snapping it in half with ease.

"How can they see us?" Akira panted, eyes wide with fear. "They only have one eye, and we have it!"

"They sense our vibrations," Talia said, never losing her smile, "they don't need to see us to know where we are."

The Graeae cackled. "We've hunted by vibrations and the whispers of the earth for centuries," Pemphredo taunted, "you can't hide from us."

Despite this revelation, we kept the eye away from them, and it clearly frustrated them. Their movements, though precise, became more desperate as their anger grew. They relied on the subtle shifts in the ground and the air, but our erratic movements were throwing them off.

Talia, seeing our predicament, made a bold move. She threw the eye high into the air, and in the moment, the Graeae looked up, she charged at them, her branch swinging in a wide arc. The blow caught them off guard, and they fell back, momentarily disoriented.

"Now, Oliver!" Talia shouted.

I didn't need to be told twice. I grabbed a large rock and, with all my strength, hurled it at the Graeae. It struck Enyo squarely in the chest, and she crumpled to the ground, unmoving. Talia followed up with a flurry of strikes, knocking Deino and Pemphredo to their knees.

Breathing heavily, I approached Talia, who was still standing over the fallen Graeae. "Is it over?" I asked, my voice shaky.

Talia shook her head. "Not yet. We have to make sure they can't come after us again."

She picked up the Graeae's eye from where it had landed and held it over her head. The remaining two Graeae watched her with a mix of fear and hatred.

"Without this eye, you're powerless," Talia said, "leave us alone, or we'll destroy it."

The Graeae hissed, but they didn't move to attack. They knew Talia wasn't bluffing.

"Go," Talia commanded, "and tell anyone who comes after us that they'll meet the same fate."

The Graeae, sensing their defeat, fell back with rage and desperation flickering in their single eye. Deino, now incapacitated, lay on the ground, while Enyo and Pemphredo clung to the last shreds of their pride. Talia stood over them, holding their eye aloft, a symbol of their downfall.

"Why do you smile, girl?" Pemphredo spat out, her voice filled with venom. "What secrets do you hide behind that cursed smile?"

Talia's smile didn't waver. "That's none of your concern," she said firmly.

I could see the tension in her posture, the slight trembling of her hand holding the eye. The Graeae's words echoed in my mind, igniting a spark of anger and suspicion. I stepped forward, unable to hold back any longer.

"Talia, why do you always smile?" I demanded, my voice rising. "Even now, after everything, you're still smiling. What are you hiding from us?"

Talia looked at me, her smile never fading. "Oliver now isn't the time-"

"No!" I interrupted, my frustration boiling over. "We deserve to know! After all we've been through together, you owe us the truth!"

The Graeae cackled weakly, savouring the discord they had sown. Enyo sneered at Talia. "Yes, tell them, girl. Tell them why you really smile. Tell them who you're really working for."

Talia's smile remained fixed, but her eyes darkened. "They're just trying to turn us against each other, don't listen to them."

But doubt gnawed at me. "Is that true, Talia? Are you hiding something from us? Are you working for someone?"

Akira looked between us, her eyes wide with confusion and fear. "Talia, please, we need to know."

Talia sighed deeply, her smile still plastered on her face. "I've always been honest with you. You have to trust me."

"How can we?" I shot back. "When you won't even stop smiling for a second, not even now."

The Graeae's laughter grew weaker as their life ebbed away. "Yes, trust her. Trust the girl who never stops smiling, who hides everything behind that grin."

In a fit of frustration and anger, I brought my rock down hard on Enyo's head. She crumpled to the ground, lifeless. Akira, taking advantage of the moment, struck Pemphredo with her branch, ending her life as well.

The forest fell silent, the only sound was our ragged breathing. Talia, still holding the eye, looked at the bodies of the Graeae with a mixture of relief and sorrow, but her smile remained.

"Are you okay?" Akira asked, her voice trembling.

Talia nodded, her smile unwavering. "I'm fine. It's over."

I looked down at the bodies, even taking the life of three old hags who wanted to kill us, left me feeling unnerved and unsettled, I could tell Akira felt it to, but Talia was the same as always, I couldn't tell what she thought about it because of that smile.

I stepped closer to her, my anger not yet spent. "Talia, you have to tell us. Why do you always smile? Are you hiding something?"

Talia looked at me, her eyes pleading. "You have to trust me, Oliver, I'm not your enemy."

"How can I when I don't feel like you're being honest? I mean look at yourself!"

- Chapter 10 -

Smiles and Suspicions

"OLIVER!" Akira yelled at me, "You can't be rude, if she's not ready don't force her!"

"No!" I yelled back, "We deserve to know, if she's going to keep helping us on this search, she's going to have to be truthful." I glared at her.

"Absolutely not!" Akira stepped in front of Talia. "Oliver, I'm your sister and I forbid you from making this poor girl do something she's clearly not ready for! If she wants to tell us she can, in her own time."

"Forbid me?" I said slowly. "You can't forbid me, you sometimes forget you're only my sister, you're not a teacher, you're not Miss Olivia or Mrs Scythe, you're not mum!"

Her eyes started to tear up, I knew I had gone way too far, she may not have been my mum but she had raised me. I felt awful, but I wasn't going to back down, I was doing it for us. Why did she want to hang on to someone who might have betrayed us?

The tension in the air crackled like lightning, each word we exchanged adding fuel to the fire. Talia stood behind Akira, her hands covering her ears, obviously sensitive to the escalating volume of our argument.

"Oliver, stop!" Akira's voice rang out, her frustration palpable. "You can't keep interrogating her like this. Talia doesn't owe us anything."

I scoffed, my patience wearing thin. "She does if she expects us to trust her, Akira. You're just too blind to see it."

Akira's eyes flashed with anger, her fists clenched at her sides. "Blind? Maybe I'm just not as paranoid as you, Oliver. Maybe I'm not constantly looking for someone to blame for our problems."

I rolled my eyes, unable to contain my sarcasm. "Well, maybe you should start, Akira. Because if you haven't noticed, our problems keep finding us, whether we're looking for them or not."

Talia flinched at the sharpness of our words, her hands pressing harder against her ears. She looked like she wanted to say something, to intervene somehow, but the intensity of our argument seemed to paralyse her.

Akira took a step forward, her gaze fierce. "You're being unreasonable, Oliver. Talia has done nothing but help us, and you're treating her like she's the enemy."

I scoffed again, my frustration boiling over. "Oh please, Akira, don't act like you're some saint defending the innocent. You're just as clueless as the rest of us."

Her jaw clenched, her patience wearing thin. "Clueless? At least I'm not so blinded by my own paranoia that I can't see when someone is trying to help us."

I sneered at her, my anger driving me to be cruel. "Oh, so now you're the expert on trust, huh? Just because you're too naive to see when someone is playing us doesn't mean I have to be."

Talia whimpered behind Akira, her hands still pressed against her ears. It was clear that the shouting was taking its toll on her, but neither of us seemed to notice, too caught up in our own anger to see the damage we were causing.

Akira's eyes flashed with hurt, her voice trembling with emotion. "I can't believe you, Oliver. I thought we were supposed to be a team, but all you care about is pushing people away."

I felt a pang of guilt at the hurt in her voice, but my pride wouldn't let me back down. "Maybe if you weren't so busy playing the martyr, you'd see that sometimes the truth hurts, Akira. And sometimes, people aren't who they say they are."

Talia let out a sob, yet still smiling, unable to bear the weight of our argument any longer. She turned and fled into the forest, her hands still pressed against her ears. I watched her go, a sinking feeling in the pit of my stomach. What had I done? What did any of that accomplish? Akira's voice broke through my thoughts, her tone laced with disappointment.

"Look what you've done, Oliver. You've driven her away." I felt a surge of anger rise within me, fuelled by shame and regret.

"Oh, don't you dare put this on me, Akira. You're the one who's always so quick to trust everyone. Maybe it's time you learned that not everyone deserves it."

With that, I turned and stormed off in the opposite direction, leaving Akira alone in the clearing. The weight of my words hung heavy in the air, a stark reminder of the damage our heated argument had caused. And as I disappeared into the forest, I couldn't shake the feeling that things were only going to get worse from here.

As the time passed I felt guiltier and guiltier, we had completely forgotten about why we were out here. I wanted to apologise, I knew deep down that I had gone too far, but Akira would thank me when I was proven right. If I was proven right.

The forest seemed to close in around me as I walked, the shadows growing longer and more menacing with each passing moment. The sounds of the forest became distant echoes, drowned out by the cacophony of my own thoughts and heavy breathing. What had I done? How could I have let my anger get the best of me, driving away the one person who had been helping us?

Guilt gnawed at me like a hungry beast, consuming me from the inside out. I knew I had to find Talia and apologise, but the thought of facing her again filled me with dread. What if she didn't want to forgive me? What if she had decided that we weren't worth the trouble after all? But one thought stayed with me, what if I was right? I looked up at the stars remembering Talia's stories and imagined what it would have been like to be there when they took place. It was hard to believe that in only a few days, I had found out that I was a son of Zeus, and that all the stories were true. I couldn't believe it, at times I didn't want to believe it. Everything was overwhelming and happening too fast and we didn't really have time to comprehend any of it properly.

As I sat there in the darkness of the forest, my heart heavy with regret and sorrow, I didn't know if I was right or not but I didn't care, I couldn't help but feel the weight of my actions bearing down on me like a crushing burden. The echoes of our argument reverberated in my mind, each harsh word a painful reminder of the rift I had created between us.

I longed to find Talia and Akira and apologise, to make things right and mend the bond that had been shattered by my own foolishness. But as the minutes turned into hours and the forest enveloped me in its silent embrace, despair threatened to consume me.

Suddenly, a soft voice broke through the stillness, filled with a mixture of anger and concern. "Oliver?" It was Akira, her voice trembling with emotion. She had been searching for me, her frustration and worry evident in the darkness.

I turned to face her, my eyes filled with tears I couldn't hold back any longer. "Akira," I whispered,

my voice choking with emotion. "I'm so sorry. I messed up. I let my anger control me, and now Talia's gone."

Akira's expression softened, her anger melting away as she saw the depth of my remorse. She knelt beside me, her hand reaching out to gently brush away my tears. "Oh, Oliver," she said, her voice trembling with sadness, "I was so angry at you, but... I can see how much you regret it now."

I nodded, unable to speak past the lump in my throat. The guilt threatened to overwhelm me, but Akira's presence was like a lifeline in the darkness, reminding me that I wasn't alone.

"We have to find Talia," she said softly, her eyes shining with determination, "we have to apologise to her and make things right. We can't let this tear us apart."

I nodded, I never liked admitting my faults but I could see this time I needed to.

As we delved deeper into the forest, the echoes of our argument reverberated through the trees like a mournful dirge, each word a dagger that pierced the already fragile bond between us. The weight of our remorse hung heavy in the air, suffocating us with its oppressive embrace, as we stumbled through the darkness in search of our lost companion.

The forest seemed to close in around us, its twisted branches reaching out like twisted, distorted claws, grasping at our fleeting hope with cruel indifference. The sounds of the night were a symphony of sorrow, a haunting melody that echoed our grief as we trudged through the dense underbrush, our hearts heavy with regret.

And then, just when it seemed like all hope was lost, we heard it. A soft, pitiful whimpering, barely audible over the mournful howling of the wind. We followed the sound, our footsteps heavy with the weight of our guilt, until we found her, huddled against the base of a tree, her slender frame trembling with silent sobs.

Talia looked up at us with tear-streaked cheeks and haunted eyes, but even in the depths of her despair, she didn't stop smiling, her lips curled upwards in a painful grimace that spoke volumes of her suffering.

My heart shattered at the sight, knowing that I was the cause of her pain. Tears pricked at my eyes as I knelt beside her, my voice barely a whisper in the stillness of the night.

"Talia," I choked out, my voice thick with sorrow. "I'm so sorry. We never should have let our anger drive us apart."

Talia's sobs grew louder, her frail form shaking with the weight of her grief. "It's not your fault," she whispered, her voice barely audible over the rustling of the leaves, "I should have been stronger. I should have told you the truth."

She looked up, her eyes shimmering with unshed tears. "I'm sorry I ran off," she said softly, "I just couldn't handle the shouting. It brought back... memories."

My guilt threatened to consume me as I reached out to touch her trembling hand. "No, Talia, it's not your fault. We... I was wrong to treat you the way I did. You've been nothing but kind to us, and I repaid you with suspicion and anger."

I looked at Akira who gave me a thumbs up, I didn't know what else to say but I knew I had to say something. I couldn't, words couldn't express how bad I felt.

Our words hung heavy in the air, a tangible reminder of the pain we had inflicted on each other. Talia's forgiveness was a balm to my wounded soul, but it couldn't erase the scars left by our heated argument.

Akira knelt beside us, her eyes filled with remorse. "I'm sorry too, Talia," she said softly, her voice trembling with emotion, "I should have stood up to Oliver sooner. I should have stopped him before things got out of hand."

Talia shook her head, her smile still strained but genuine. "It's not your fault, Akira. You were just trying to protect me. I should have been more honest with you both from the beginning."

I nodded, my throat tight with emotion. "We all made mistakes," I admitted, my voice barely above a whisper, "but we can't change the past. All we can do is learn from it and try to do better in the future."

But the question was still eating away at me, why did she always smile? During the battle, whilst crying. I didn't want to ask, because that's what caused her to run off, the argument.

We stayed there until the sun came up, and we must've fallen asleep at one point as I woke up to a loud noise.

I led up and grabbed my branch, ready to attack and defend.

"Hey kid, calm down," a man stepped into view, he had a blonde mullet and a worn-out leather jacket.

I took a defensive stance, my heart racing with adrenaline as the man stepped into view. He was just an ordinary-looking guy, with a friendly smile and a casual demeanour that seemed out of place in the midst of the forest. "Who are you?" I demanded, my voice tense with suspicion.

"What do you want?"

The man held up his hands in a placating gesture, his smile never wavering. "Easy there, kid. I didn't mean to startle you. My name's Jake. I was just out for a morning hike when I heard some commotion and came to check it out."

I relaxed slightly, but I still kept my guard up. "Commotion?"

"Yeah, sounded like someone was in trouble," Jake said, his brow furrowing with concern, "I figured I'd see if I could lend a hand."

I glanced over at Talia and Akira, still sleeping peacefully in the tent, I hoped he wouldn't notice the Graeae eye that was sitting next to the backpack, or the sword. It would be hard to explain them. "We're fine," I said gruffly, not wanting to reveal too much to a stranger. "We don't need any help."

Jake nodded, understanding evident in his eyes. "Fair enough, sorry for intruding. I'll just be on my way then."

As he turned to leave, a thought occurred to me. "Wait!" I called out, stopping him in his tracks.

"Have you seen anything... unusual around here? Like, I don't know, strange creatures or...

anything out of the ordinary?"

Jake raised an eyebrow, a hint of amusement in his eyes. "You mean besides the fact that we're in the middle of a forest?" he joked. "No, can't say I have but if you're looking for trouble, I'd steer clear of those caves up ahead. They've got a bit of a reputation."

I frowned, the mention of caves sending a shiver down my spine, but maybe they were the caves we were looking for. "Thanks for the warning," I said, my tone wary, "we'll keep that in mind."

Jake gave me a nod and a wave before disappearing into the forest, leaving me alone with my thoughts. As I watched him go, I couldn't shake the feeling that there was more to him than met the eye. But for now, I had more pressing concerns. I needed to wake Talia and Akira, and together, we had to figure out our next move.

- Chapter 11 -

Unveiling the Past

We started heading towards the caves, I couldn't keep my eyes off Talia, I was still wanting to ask about her smile but I couldn't bring myself to. I walked behind her with Akira standing next to me, "So... Talia, what are you going to do when you see your mum?"

She looked back at us, "I don't know."

Akira and I stared at each other, she didn't know?

"It's complicated."

I was confused. She was so eager to join us on the quest to find her mother but she didn't know what she would do when she found her, in fact, I didn't know anything about Talia, she was like an enigma to me.

"When was the last time you saw her?"

Talia stopped in her tracks, her face one of confusion as if she was trying to remember, "About six years ago, maybe longer."

"Oh?" I muttered, I thought they would have been quite close, "That's a long time."

Talia nodded, her expression clouded with a mixture of sadness and determination. "Yes, it is but she's all I've got left. Finding her is the only thing that keeps me going."

Akira and I exchanged a look, her eyes reflecting the same uncertainty and concern I felt. We had been on this quest together, but there was still so much we didn't know about Talia, her past, and the true motivations driving her.

As we walked, the forest seemed to grow thicker, the trees closing in around us as if guiding us towards our destination. The air grew cooler, the shadows lengthening as we continued. My mind raced with questions and doubts, but one thing remained clear: we had to press on.

Hours passed, and our steps grew slower, the weight of exhaustion bearing down on us. The day's events had taken their toll, leaving us drained and weary. The thick underbrush and uneven terrain made our journey even more gruelling, each step a reminder of how vulnerable we were.

Akira stumbled, her foot catching on a root, and I instinctively reached out to steady her. "We need to rest," I said, my voice firm but gentle. "We're all exhausted. We won't make it to the caves if we push ourselves too hard."

She nodded in agreement, her face pale with fatigue. "Oliver's right. Let's find a safe spot to camp for the night."

Reluctantly, Talia agreed, her eyes heavy with weariness. We found a small clearing sheltered by towering trees, the ground covered in a soft layer of moss. It was a quiet, peaceful spot, a stark contrast to the turmoil within us.

As we set up camp, the flickering light of our small fire casting long shadows on the surrounding trees, I couldn't shake the feeling that we were being watched. The forest seemed to hold its breath, the night alive with the whispers of unseen eyes. I kept my suspicions to myself, not wanting to add to our collective anxiety.

We sat in a circle around the fire, the warmth a welcome comfort against the chill of the night. Talia's gaze was distant, her thoughts clearly elsewhere. I watched her, the questions I had been too afraid to ask swirling in my mind.

Suddenly, she turned to me, her eyes piercing through the darkness. "I can feel you thinking, Oliver," she said, her voice echoing in the stillness, "your doubts, your questions - they're like a storm raging inside you."

Her words struck me like a bolt of lightning, the raw intensity in her eyes sending shivers down my spine.

"Talia," I began, my voice barely above a whisper, "why do you always smile? Even when you're in pain, even when you're crying—why?"

The words came pouring out before I could stop them, this time though they sounded like a genuine question rather than an accusation.

"I don't want to hurt you or make you feel uncomfortable," I hurriedly added softly, trying to find the right words to say, "but there are so many questions we don't have the answer to, maybe if you tell us we can help."

Talia's eyes widened in surprise, then softened with a mix of sorrow and resolve. She took a deep breath, and for a moment, the only sound was the crackling of the fire. The flickering flames cast a warm glow on her face, but it did little to mask the shadows in her eyes.

"My smile," she began, her voice steady but tinged with an underlying sadness, "is not what it seems. It's not joy or happiness. It's a shield, a mask I wear to protect myself from the world."

She paused, her gaze dropping to the ground as if gathering her thoughts. Akira and I sat in silence, the weight of her words hanging in the air.

"I suppose I should start from the beginning," Talia said, her voice barely above a whisper.

"My mother, Nemesis, met my father, Rich Mallory, under circumstances that were anything but ordinary. He was drawn to her strength, her power, but he didn't know the truth about her divine nature. When I was born, they both hoped for a normal family life, or at least something resembling it, but you know gods and mortals wanting something normal, that's impossible."

Talia's eyes grew distant, her mind clearly wandering back to painful memories. "But it didn't take long for my father to realise that I wasn't just an ordinary child. That's when my mother had to reveal the truth about herself and that I was a demigod, and that terrified him. He couldn't accept what I represented. He saw me as a curse, a regret he couldn't escape from. When he realised my mother was a goddess he wanted nothing to do with her. He blamed her for everything, saying it was all her fault, then after she left, he started to blame me."

I felt a pang of guilt and sorrow at her words, realising the depth of her suffering.

"Is that why he named you Rue?" Akira asked softly.

Talia nodded, her expression pained. "Yes. Rue means regret, and that's what he felt for having me. My last name, Mallory, means unlucky. He often said he was unlucky to be stuck with me. My mother named me Talia, but my father insisted on the middle name Rue as a constant reminder of his regret."

She swallowed hard, the raw emotion in her eyes making it clear how deeply this hurt her. "For a while, my mother and I tried to make things work, but it was impossible. My father's resentment only grew stronger. He stopped caring for me, and the visits from Nemesis and Nyx became less frequent until they stopped altogether. I was just a burden to him, a reminder of his mistakes."

Talia's voice broke slightly, and she took a moment to compose herself. "When I was six, my father sent me away to live with Nemesis, hoping to rid himself of me. We were supposed to meet at camp, but Nemesis never showed up. I've been living at the camp ever since, trying to make sense of my life, trying to find my place in a world that seems to have no room for someone like me."

Tears welled up in her eyes, but her smile remained, a painful testament to her resilience. "I learned three things that day," she continued, her voice growing stronger, "firstly, I wasn't going to let anyone see that they got to me again. My smile became my armour, a way to hide my pain and keep others at a distance. Secondly, I realised that I couldn't rely on anyone but myself. Trusting others only led to heartbreak and disappointment."

She paused, looking directly at me, her eyes burning with a fierce determination. "And thirdly, I vowed that no matter how much it hurt, no matter how much I wanted to give up, I would keep going. I would find my mother, I would find my place, and I would prove that I am more than just a regret or a burden."

Her words hung in the air, heavy with the weight of her suffering and her resolve. I felt a lump in my throat, my heart aching for the girl who had endured so much pain and still found the strength to keep going.

"Talia," I said softly, my voice thick with emotion, "I had no idea. I'm so sorry for everything you've been through. And for how I treated you. I let my own fears and suspicions cloud my judgement."

Akira reached out, placing a comforting hand on Talia's shoulder. "We're here for you, Talia. We'll find your mother, and we'll do it together. You're not alone anymore."

Talia's smile softened, a glimmer of genuine warmth breaking through the pain. "Thank you," she whispered, "it means more than you know."

We sat there in the silence of the forest, the fire

crackling softly as the night enveloped us. In that moment, a fragile bond was formed, forged through shared pain and the promise of a brighter future. And as we sat together, the darkness seemed a little less oppressive, the shadows a little less daunting. We had each other, and for now, that was enough.

Talia broke the silence. "Well, what about you two?"

I looked at Akira who looked back at me.

"Huh?"

"What's the deal with you two? It's pretty obvious you guys went through something."

Akira sighed, her eyes reflecting a deep-seated pain. "We did, when I was eight and Oliver was five, our lives changed forever. It was a stormy night, the kind where the wind howls and lightning splits the sky. Our mother, Carrie, was driving us home. The rain was coming down in sheets, making it nearly impossible to see the road."

Akira's voice trembled as she continued. "We were on a winding road, the kind that hugs the side of a cliff. The storm was relentless, and visibility was next to nothing. Mum was trying to stay calm, but I could see the fear in her eyes. I remember looking out the window and seeing a flash of lightning that seemed to light up the entire world." She paused, her eyes distant as if she were reliving the moment. "Then it happened: a car coming from the opposite direction swerved into our lane. Mum tried to avoid it, but the road was slick with rain. She lost control of the car, and we went off the road."

I could feel the tension in the air as Akira spoke, the memories clearly haunting her. "The car tumbled down the embankment, crashing through trees and rocks. I remember the sound of metal crunching, glass shattering, and then... darkness. When I came to, I was in pain, but all I could think about was Oliver. I had been sitting in the back with him, and somehow, I managed to shield him with my body."

She pointed to her scar, "That's how I got this."

Her voice broke, and I reached out to squeeze her hand, offering silent support. "Our mother didn't survive," she said softly, "Oliver and I were trapped in that car, surrounded by the wreckage of our lives. The smell of gasoline, the sight of our mother's lifeless body—it's something that never leaves you."

Talia listened intently, her eyes filled with empathy. "I'm so sorry," she whispered, "I can't imagine what that must have been like."

Akira nodded, tears glistening in her eyes. "Eventually, a police car found us. They pulled us out and took us to a hospital. We had nowhere to go after that, no family who could take us in. So, we ended up in a boarding school."

The memories of that time were etched into my mind like scars on my soul. The loneliness, the bullying, the feeling of being unwanted.

"The school took us in for free at first," Akira continued. "But most people there, including all the teachers except for one, didn't like us. They made us feel like we were a burden, nuisances. As soon as I turned thirteen, I had to get three part-time evening jobs just to pay for our living expenses. No other child had to go through that. Their parents paid for everything. But for us, it was different."

"We got bullied," Akira continued, her voice tinged with a mix of anger and sadness. "Talia, you knew from going to school with us before. It was relentless. But we had no choice. We had nowhere else to go."

Talia's eyes were filled with tears, her heart clearly aching for us. "I'm so sorry," she whispered, her voice thick with emotion. "I had no idea you went through so much."

Akira nodded, her eyes glistening with unshed tears. "We survived because we had each other, unlike you who had to shoulder everything on your own."

But it wasn't easy, and sometimes, it feels like the weight of those years will never fully go away."

"When did you find out about your half brother? At camp?" I asked quizzically.

Talia spoke softly and mournfully " that's a story for another time"

The silence that followed was heavy with unspoken words, the weight of our shared pain and the bonds that had formed through our collective suffering. Talia reached out, her hand resting gently on mine. "Thank you for sharing that with me," she said softly. "I understand a little more now. We're all carrying our own burdens, but maybe we can help each other bear them."

I nodded, feeling a sense of relief wash over me. For the first time in a long while, I felt like we weren't alone. We had Talia, and she had us. And together, maybe we could find the strength to face whatever challenges lay ahead.

As the fire crackled softly in the darkness, we sat together, the night closing in around us. In that moment, we were united by our shared pain and our determination to move forward. It felt as if there was a bond of friendship that had unified us, a bond that felt stronger than anything than Akira and I ever had with anyone else.

The night wore on, the flames of the fire gradually dwindling as exhaustion began to weigh heavily upon us. The events of the day had taken their toll, leaving us drained both physically and emotionally. But despite our weariness, sleep remained elusive, our minds were still plagued by the ghosts of our pasts.

I lay on my back, staring up at the canopy of stars overhead, each twinkle a reminder of the vastness of the universe and the insignificance of our troubles in the grand scheme of things. I tried to find solace in the beauty of the night sky.

Akira lay beside me, her breathing steady and even, but I could tell from the tension in her muscles that sleep eluded her as well. We had shared our pasts with Talia, laying bare the wounds that still haunted us, but the scars ran deep, and the memories lingered like shadows in the darkness.

Talia slept fitfully across from us, her brow furrowed in troubled dreams. I wanted to reach out to her, to offer some measure of comfort, but I knew that the demons she faced were her own to conquer. All I could do was be there for her when she needed me, just as she had been there for us.

The fire crackled softly, casting flickering shadows across the forest floor. In its dim glow, I felt a sense of peace wash over me and a sense of ease of understanding. We three had been thrown together in this quest but we were more alike than I would have ever imagined, a fleeting respite from the turmoil of our journey. But even as I closed my eyes and let the darkness embrace me, I knew that the trials that lay ahead would test us in ways we could scarcely imagine.

As sleep finally claimed me, I whispered a silent prayer to whatever gods might be listening, asking for strength and courage to face the challenges that awaited us. I drifted in and out of dreams, I knew that no matter what trials lay ahead, we would face them together, bound by the bonds of friendship and the shared determination to forge our own destiny.

But little did I know that the night held one final cruel twist of fate. In the depths of my dreams, I found myself transported back to that stormy night so many years ago, reliving the horror of the accident that had torn our family apart.

I watched helplessly as our mother's car careened off the road, the sound of metal crunching and glass shattering echoing in my ears like a symphony of despair. I reached out to her, screaming her name into the darkness, but she was gone, lost to me forever.

Tears streamed down my cheeks as I relived the moment of impact, the sensation of the car tumbling down the embankment like a rollercoaster ride from hell. I felt the crushing weight of the wreckage pressing down on me, suffocating me with its unyielding grip.

And then, just as suddenly as it had begun, the nightmare ended, leaving me gasping for breath and drenched in a cold sweat. I lay there in the darkness, trembling with fear and grief, the memory of that fateful night burning like a brand on my soul but found Talia by my side holding my hand.

As dawn broke on the horizon, I knew that the scars of the past would never truly heal, that the pain would always linger just beneath the surface, waiting to resurface at the slightest provocation. But even in the midst of my despair, I clung to the hope that someday, somehow, we would find the peace and redemption we so desperately sought.

But for now, all we could do was press on, one step at a time, guided by the flickering light of the fire and the promise of a new day. And as we rose to face the challenges that lay ahead, I knew that no matter what trials awaited us, we would face them together, bound by the unbreakable bonds of love and loss that had forged us into the people we were meant to be.

The first light of dawn began to filter through the trees, casting a soft golden glow over the forest. As Akira woke from her slumber, I could feel the tension of past traumas slightly lifted, our opening up had seemed to be the first part of all of our healing and a new feeling of hopefulness seemed apparent. The resilience that Talia portrayed was inspiring though I did wonder if finding her mother would give her the closure she so desperately sought.

Akira sat beside me, her eyes bleary with exhaustion. She reached out, grasping my hand in hers with a silent understanding that spoke volumes. We were in this together, we needed to focus on our future and for the time being, that was the quest.

We prepared for our journey with a sense of relief among us, that heavy weight seemed to have been lifted from all of our shoulders, even the thought of unknown challenges that lay ahead didn't seem to hold the same fear and the atmosphere seemed to be more relaxed. We were combined in the determination for answers and hopefully, some peace we all desperately sought. With a final glance back at the campsite, we set off once more into the unknown, our footsteps echoing through the quiet stillness of the forest. And as we disappeared into the dense undergrowth, I knew that no matter what trials awaited us, we would face them with courage and resilience, guided by the flickering light of hope that burned brightly within each of us.

- Chapter 12 -

The River Lethe

The forest canopy above us thickened as we pressed onward, casting long shadows that danced in the early morning light. The air was cool and crisp, a refreshing change from the cold frost of the previous day. With beams of sunlight pushing their way through the thick canopy. Talia led the way, her movements purposeful and determined, while Akira and I followed closely behind. The banter was light hearted and both Akira and Talia laughed at my jokes, although I wasn't sure Talia really understood them, though it was nice to see her more... normal. The dense underbrush and uneven terrain made each step a challenge, but we persevered, driven by the promise of reaching the caves that held the answers we sought.

As we trekked deeper into the forest, an unfamiliar scent began to waft through the air. It was sweet and enticing, unlike anything I had ever smelled before. The aroma was almost intoxicating, stirring a deep sense of curiosity within me. I glanced at Akira, who seemed equally intrigued by the mysterious fragrance.

"Do you smell that?" I asked, my voice hushed with wonder.

Akira nodded, her eyes widening as she inhaled deeply. "Yeah, it smells... amazing. Like the sweetest flowers mixed with something I can't quite place."

Talia, who was a few steps ahead, turned to face us. Her expression, usually so guarded, softened with a trace of concern. "We need to be careful," she said, her voice laced with urgency, "stay close and don't touch anything."

We nodded, though I couldn't help but feel a twinge of scepticism. The scent was so inviting, so alluring, that it was hard to imagine anything dangerous associated with it. Nevertheless, we continued onward, our senses heightened and our eyes scanning the surroundings for any signs of danger.

As we emerged from the thick underbrush, we found ourselves standing on the edge of a wide, shimmering river. The water sparkled in the sunlight, its surface so clear that it seemed to glow with an ethereal light. The scent that had been teasing our senses emanated from the river, growing stronger and more enticing the closer we got.

"This is incredible," Akira breathed, her eyes fixed on the water. "I've never seen anything like it."

Without a second thought, I stepped forward, drawn by the mesmerising flow of the river. The water looked so pure, so inviting, that I felt an almost irresistible urge to reach out and touch it. My mind clouded by the intoxicating scent, I found myself bending down, my hand outstretched towards the shimmering surface.

Just as my fingers were about to touch the water, Talia's hand shot out and grabbed my arm, pulling me back with surprising force. "Oliver, no!" she exclaimed, her voice a mix of fear and urgency.

I blinked, the spell of the river momentarily broken. "What? Why?" I stammered, confused by her sudden reaction.

"This... this is the River Lethe," Talia said, her voice barely above a whisper, "we can't touch it, let alone drink from it."

"The River Lethe?" Akira echoed, confusion etching her features. "What's so special about it?"

Talia took a deep breath, her grip on my arm still firm. "The River Lethe is one of the five rivers of the Underworld. It's also known as the River of Forgetfulness. If you drink from it or even touch the water, you will forget everything - your name, how to eat, how to breathe. Eventually, you will forget how to live."

A cold chill ran through me at her words, the enchanting beauty of the river suddenly taking on a sinister edge. "Forget everything?" I repeated, the gravity of the situation sinking in. "That's... terrifying."

The scent of the river grew stronger, its sweet, seductive aroma clouding my thoughts once more. Despite Talia's warning, an overwhelming urge to drink the water washed over me. I found myself leaning forward again, my mind foggy and my hand trembling with desire.

"Oliver, stop!" Akira's voice rang out, sharp and clear. She grabbed my other arm, pulling me back just as my fingers grazed the water's surface. The sudden jolt snapped me out of the river's spell, and I stumbled back, my heart pounding in my chest.

Talia's expression was tense, her eyes darting back and forth as if searching for something unseen. "We need to get away from here," she said, her voice steady but urgent. "The scent is meant to lure you in, to make you want to drink from it. But we must resist."

I took a step back, my earlier curiosity now replaced by a deep sense of unease. The river that had seemed so inviting just moments ago now felt like a trap, its beauty hiding a deadly secret. Akira moved closer to me, her expression mirroring my own unease.

"So, how do we get across?" I asked, my mind racing with the implications of Talia's revelation.

Talia shook her head, her gaze sweeping the riverbank. "We'll have to find another way. There might be a bridge or a narrow spot where we can jump across. But under no circumstances should we touch the water."

As we began to search for a safe crossing point, I couldn't help but feel a lingering sense of dread. The River Lethe, with its deceptive beauty and deadly allure, was a stark reminder of the dangers that lay ahead. And though we had been warned, the intoxicating scent continued to tease our senses, a constant temptation that we had to fight against with every step.

"Wait! You said it was one of the five underworld rivers, underworld. How is it here?" Akira asked.

"All the underworld rivers meet up at some point, every river in the world connects to at least one of them, some even meet up with all of them," she explained.

We moved cautiously along the riverbank, the sweet aroma of the water growing stronger with each passing moment. I glanced at Akira, who seemed equally affected by the scent, her eyes glazed with a mix of curiosity and wariness. It was as if the river was calling out to us, whispering promises of peace and forgetfulness that were hard to ignore.

Talia led the way, her eyes scanning the surroundings for any sign of a safe crossing. Her determination was unwavering, her focus sharp as she navigated the treacherous terrain. I admired her strength and resilience, even as I struggled to keep my own thoughts in check.

"Look!" Akira said suddenly, pointing ahead. "There's a fallen tree over there. Maybe we can use it to cross."

We hurried to the spot she had indicated, finding a large tree that had toppled over, its trunk stretching across the river like a natural bridge. The sight filled me with a sense of relief, though the ever-present scent of the river served as a constant reminder of the danger that lay beneath.

Talia approached the fallen tree cautiously, testing its stability with a careful step. "This might work," she said, her voice steady. "But we need to be extremely careful. One slip, and we could fall into the water."

We nodded in agreement, the gravity of her words sinking in. One by one, we began to cross the makeshift bridge, our movements slow and deliberate. The tree trunk was wide enough to walk on, but the thought of what lay below kept us on edge, our senses heightened with fear and determination.

As I carefully made my way across, the scent of the river seemed to intensify, filling my nostrils with its sweet, intoxicating aroma. I could feel its pull, a gentle tug at the edges of my consciousness, urging me to let go and succumb to its allure. But I forced myself to focus, my grip tightening on the rough bark beneath my feet.

Halfway across, I glanced down at the shimmering water below, a shiver running through me at the sight. The river was beautiful, its surface glistening like liquid silver in the sunlight. But I knew the danger it held, the deadly promise of oblivion that awaited anyone who dared to touch its depths.

Talia was the first to reach the other side, her movements quick and sure as she stepped onto solid ground. She turned to face us, her eyes filled with a mixture of relief and urgency. "Hurry," she called out, her voice carrying over the gentle murmur of the river.

Akira followed next, her steps steady and confident despite the danger below. I watched her closely, my heart pounding in my chest as she made her way across. When she finally reached the other side, a wave of relief washed over me, knowing that she was safe.

Taking a deep breath, I continued my own crossing, each step a careful balance between fear and determination. The scent of the river seemed to grow stronger with every moment, its sweet, seductive aroma clouding my thoughts and testing my resolve. Halfway across, I glanced down at the shimmering water below, a shiver running down my spine as I remembered Talia's warning. The memory of her words echoed in my mind, a stark reminder of the danger we faced.

Suddenly, the world around me began to blur, the edges of my vision growing hazy as the scent of the river seemed to penetrate my very being. I felt a strange, disorienting sensation, as if I were being pulled into a different time and place. The forest around me faded away, replaced by a vivid, haunting memory from my past.

I was back in our small, modest home, the one we had lived in before everything changed. The walls were painted a cheerful yellow, the furniture worn but comfortable. I could hear the sound of rain pattering against the windows. Mum was in the kitchen, her back to me as she prepared dinner. The smell of spaghetti sauce filled the air, a comforting scent that contrasted sharply with the tension in the room. I could hear her talking on the phone, her voice filled with a mix of anger and desperation.

"You can't just abandon them!" she exclaimed, her voice cracking with emotion. "They're your children, too. You have a responsibility."

I knew she was talking to our father, Zeus, the god we had never met. The god who had never been there for us. Mum had always spoken of him with a mix of reverence and bitterness, a man of immense power who chose to stay distant from his mortal children. Though she never said who he was, his name or why he left.

The argument continued, her voice growing louder and more heated. I stood in the doorway, feeling helpless and afraid, unable to do anything but watch as my mother struggled with the weight of raising two demi-god children on her own.

The memory shifted, and suddenly I was back in the car, the storm raging outside as mum drove us home. Akira and I sat in the backseat, our hands tightly clasped together as we watched the world blur by in a haze of rain and darkness.

"Everything's going to be okay," Mum said, her voice filled with a calm determination that belied the fear in her eyes. "We're going to get through this."

But even as she spoke, I could see the strain in her expression, the worry lines etched into her face. I knew that things were far from okay, the storm brewing outside was loud and frightening to the younger version of me. The memory faded, and I found myself back on the fallen tree trunk, the scent of the River Lethe still lingering in the air. My heart was pounding in my chest, my mind reeling from the intensity of the flashback. I took a deep breath, trying to steady myself as I continued my precarious journey across the river.

Finally, with a sense of relief that bordered on euphoria, I reached the other side, my feet touching solid ground once more. Talia and Akira were waiting for me, their expressions filled with concern. "Are you okay?" Talia asked, her voice gentle.

I nodded, still trying to shake off the remnants of the memory that had gripped me so fiercely.

"Yeah, I'm fine," I said, though my voice sounded hollow even to my own ears.

Talia reached out, placing a reassuring hand on my shoulder. "That river has a way of dredging up memories we'd rather forget," she said softly. "But you made it across. That's what matters."

I forced a smile, though I knew it didn't reach my eyes. "Thanks," I said, grateful for her understanding.

We stood there for a moment, the weight of our mutual experiences hanging heavy in the air. Despite the danger we had faced, there was a sense of solidarity between us, a bond forged through adversity and strengthened by our determination to overcome it.

With a final glance back at the River Lethe, we continued our journey deeper into the forest, our footsteps echoing in the quiet stillness of the morning. And though the memory of the river's deadly allure lingered, I tried to push it to the back of my mind, I knew that we would press on, united by our shared purpose and the unbreakable bonds of friendship that now held us together.

As we continued our journey through the forest, the memories stirred by the River Lethe where like a hard pill to swallow but I didn't want to be drawn back into the sad memories of my past but remember the happier times, I did want to ask Akira if she had experienced the same sort of recollection of past events as she crossed the river as I did, though I also want to tell her how much I appreciated everything she had done for me and still does without complaint.

I decided to stop thinking about the memories I could have lost, they were still here, they were safe. I won't forget them. I sped up and walked beside Akira.

"When you were crossing the Lethe, were your thoughts old memories?" I asked her, if they were horrible memories we wanted to forget that they brought to our mind, what was she thinking about? The same things as me? Or was it me?

"Yeah, mum, school, dad."

"Dad?" I asked, we had never met him, had we? Was I too young to remember?

"The last time he visited, it was just before you were born. I remembered he was tall and strong but he could be fierce. I was young, I don't remember much but I do remember their raised voices, mum being upset and him never coming back after that. As I got older, I just assumed that his job took him away a lot, that's why they fell out and maybe he left to start a new family. It never occurred to me he was the King of the Gods."

As we continued our journey through the forest, the path seemed to stretch endlessly before us, each step taking us further from the River Lethe and the memories it had stirred. I refused to allow the lingering effects of the river's enchantment to remain and cast a shadow on our future thoughts and conversation.

As we walked, it was harder than I thought to shake the feeling of unease that had settled over me since our encounter with the River Lethe. The memories it had dredged up lingered in the back of my mind like spectres refusing to be banished. I glanced at Talia, wondering what thoughts had plagued her during our crossing of the deadly river.

"Talia," I began, my voice hesitant, "what memories did the River Lethe bring to mind for you? If you don't mind sharing, that is."

Talia's gaze drifted to the forest floor, her expression distant as she seemed to delve into the recesses of her mind. "The River Lethe," she murmured, her voice barely above a whisper. "It brought back memories of... loss. Loss and longing."

I exchanged a concerned glance with Akira, sensing the weight of Talia's words. "What kind of loss?" Akira asked gently, her voice soft with understanding.

Talia took a deep breath, her eyes clouded with sorrow. "The loss of my childhood," she said, her voice tinged with bitterness, "the loss of innocence, of family, of a sense of belonging. The River Lethe reminded me of all that I've had to sacrifice, all that I've had to endure."

My heart ached for Talia, for the pain and loneliness she had experienced at such a young age. "I'm so sorry, Talia," I said softly, reaching out to place a comforting hand on her shoulder. "You've been through so much."

Talia offered me a small, sad smile, her eyes shimmering with unshed tears. "Thank you," she said, her voice barely above a whisper, "but I've learned to carry my burdens with me, to use them as fuel to keep moving forward. The River Lethe may have tried to steal my memories, but some things are too deeply ingrained to ever be forgotten."

"Well that was... definitely something, I knew there would be danger, but a river, really? That's not exactly what I had in mind."

"Yeah me neither," Akira agreed.

"Well hey, it could always be worse right? Imagine it was the phlegethon, I do not feel like bathing in fire today. No Sir, not for me."

- Chapter 13 -

The Cave

The forest habitat took a strange turn, from the hundreds of trees and the density of the canopies, with a cacophony of animal and bird noises to thorny vines and a black trail that snaked its way in and out forming an unwelcoming path, there was an eerie quietness, I could no longer hear the sounds of forest creatures that had seemed to be travelling with us on our journey. The air felt thick and I found it hard to breathe, the air didn't feel fresh, more like humid and as if we were breathing in a dense fog. We had been moving slowly through the thorny trail in silence, when Talia let out a whisper of excitement

"We are close, I know we are, I can feel it."

"Great!" I muttered, pulling out another thorn that had somehow managed to cling to my arm.

"All I can feel are these damn thorns, I feel like a hedgehog."

As we pressed onward, the air grew heavy with a sense of anticipation, the promise of discovery hanging thick in the air. We knew that somewhere within these woods lay the entrance to the cave where Nyx and Nemesis resided, and our determination to find them only grew stronger with each step.

Finally, after what felt like hours of trudging through the dense undergrowth, and me feeling like a human pin cushion, we stumbled upon a narrow, rocky path leading deeper into the forest. The path was overgrown with tangled vines and moss-covered rocks, but it seemed to beckon us forward with an irresistible allure. Without a word, we followed its winding course, our expectation building with each twist and turn.

As we rounded a particularly sharp bend in the path, the trees suddenly parted, revealing a gaping black maw in the side of a towering cliff. The entrance to the cave loomed before us, its yawning darkness a stark contrast to the dappled light of the forest. I felt a shiver run down my spine as I gazed into the depths of the cavern, a sense of foreboding settling over me like a heavy cloak.

Talia stepped forward, her movements steady and sure despite the trepidation written on her face. "This is it," she said, her voice barely above a whisper. "The entrance to Nyx and Nemesis' cave."

Akira and I exchanged a nervous glance, our hearts pounding in our chests as we prepared to venture into the unknown. With a deep breath, I tightened my grip on the torch in my hand and followed Talia into the darkness.

The cave was vast, its rocky walls stretching up into the darkness overhead. The air was cool and musty, tinged with the scent of damp earth and ancient stone. As our torch flickered to life, casting long shadows that danced across the cavern walls, I couldn't help but feel a sense of awe and wonder at the sheer size and grandeur of our surroundings.

We moved deeper into the cave, our footsteps echoing in the quiet darkness. The ground beneath our feet was uneven and rocky, making each step a precarious balance between progress and stumbling. But despite the obstacles that lay before us, our determination to find Nyx and Nemesis never wavered.

As we ventured further into the heart of the cave, the darkness seemed to grow thicker around us, swallowing up the feeble light of our torch and leaving us to navigate by touch alone. I could feel the dampness of the stone, the taste of the earthy damp air, I could feel the weight of the shadows pressing in on all sides, a suffocating presence that threatened to engulf us at any moment.

Suddenly, without warning, the ground beneath us gave way, sending us tumbling into a dark abyss below. I cried out in alarm as I fell, the sound of my voice echoing off the cavern walls as if mocking my fear. I reached out blindly, searching for something, anything to grab onto, but my hands found only empty air.

Just when I thought all was lost, I felt a strong hand close around my wrist, pulling me back from the brink of what felt like oblivion, I was now back on terra ferma. It was Talia, thank the gods, her face a mask of determination as she struggled to haul me back to safety. With a final, desperate effort, she managed to drag me onto solid ground, where I lay gasping for breath, my heart pounding in my chest.

"Are you okay?" Akira's voice rang out through the darkness, filled with concern.

I nodded weakly, still trying to catch my breath.

"Yeah," I managed to say, my voice barely above a whisper. I was sure that maybe in the future I would say it was better than any rollercoaster ride that I had been on, but I was just glad I was in one piece.

Talia helped me to my feet, her grip firm and reassuring. "We need to be more careful," she said, her voice stern. "This cave is full of hidden dangers. We can't afford to let our guard down."

With a renewed sense of caution, we pressed onward, our torch casting a feeble light that barely penetrated the thick darkness surrounding us. The walls of the cave seemed to close in around us, their rocky contours twisting and turning in a bewildering maze of tunnels and passages.

Despite the oppressive darkness and the ever-present sense of danger, there was a strange beauty to the cave that I couldn't help but admire. The walls were lined with glittering crystals that caught the light of our torch and cast shimmering rainbows across the cavern walls. Stalactites hung from the ceiling like jagged teeth, their pointed tips glistening with moisture.

As we continued our search for Nyx and Nemesis, the cave seemed to stretch on endlessly before us, its twisting passages leading us deeper into the heart of the earth. We passed through vast chambers filled with strange rock formations and eerie shadows, each step bringing us closer to our elusive quarry.

But despite our best efforts, there was no sign of either Nyx or Nemesis. The cave seemed to be deserted, its silent halls echoing with the emptiness of our footsteps. I couldn't help but feel a sense of frustration and disappointment, knowing that we had come so far only to be met with another dead end.

And then, just when it seemed that all hope was lost, we stumbled upon a hidden chamber nestled deep within the bowels of the cave. The chamber was unlike anything we had seen before, its walls adorned with intricate carvings and strange symbols that seemed to pulsate with an otherworldly energy.

At the heart of the chamber stood a towering statue of Nyx, her dark form looming over us like a silent guardian. Her eyes seemed to follow us as we moved through the chamber, their piercing gaze filled with an ancient wisdom that sent shivers down my spine.

"This must be where Nyx and Nemesis reside," Talia said, her voice hushed with admiration, "but where are they?"

Before any of us could answer, the torch in my hand suddenly flickered and died, plunging us into total darkness. Oh gods no, not again, nothing good ever happens when the lights go out, I saw the movies. I felt a chill run down my spine as the shadows closed in around us, their suffocating embrace sending a wave of fear coursing through my veins.

"We need to find another source of light," Akira said, her voice urgent, "quickly, before the darkness consumes us."

I fumbled blindly through the darkness, searching desperately for anything that could help us escape. And then, just as all hope seemed lost, my hand closed around something cold and metallic at the bottom of Akira's bag. A flashlight.

With a trembling hand, I flicked the switch, sending a beam of light cutting through the darkness like a knife. The chamber was bathed in its brilliant glow, revealing every detail with crystal clarity.

But as the light washed over the walls of the cave, something strange happened. The carvings and symbols seemed to come alive, their ancient forms shifting and changing before our eyes. And then, with a sudden, blinding flash of light, everything went dark once more.

I blinked in confusion, my heart pounding in my chest as I tried to make sense of what had just happened.

"It's Nyx," I heard Talia's voice say somewhere close to me, "she's the Goddess of the Night."

"Great... just great," I muttered, "how are we meant to see anything?"

"We don't."

"Then how are we meant to find Nemesis if she is here?"

"And get out," Akira said.

The darkness seemed to press in on us like a physical force, stifling our movements and clouding our thoughts. But even in the midst of the suffocating blackness, I could feel a strange sense of clarity washing over me, as if the darkness itself held the answers we sought.

"We need to trust in ourselves," Talia said, her voice steady despite the ambivalence that hung in the air, "we have to find a way out of here, we are on the right path I know it."

With an unwavering sense of resolve, we pressed onward, our footsteps echoing off the cavern walls as we moved deeper into the heart of the chamber. I felt the burden of accountability, ensuring we fulfilled the quest in finding Nemesis for all our sakes no matter our individual agendas for doing so but the pressure of both Akira and Talia's safety lay heavily on my mind.

Suddenly, a faint glow appeared in the darkness ahead, drawing us forward like moths to a flame.

As we drew closer, the glow resolved itself into a shimmering pool of moonlight, its silvery surface rippling with an otherworldly energy.

"It's beautiful," Akira whispered, her voice filled with wonder.

"It's a sign," I said, my voice filled with hope, "...a sign that we're on the right path."

With a sense of awe and determination, we stepped into the pool of moonlight, its cool embrace washing over us like a gentle caress. I felt a strange sense of peace settle over me as I gazed up at the cavern ceiling, where the faint outline of a crescent moon shimmered in the darkness.

"This way," Talia said, her voice cutting through the silence like a knife.

As we continued onwards through the cavernous tunnels, the temperature dropped. I looked at both Akira and Talia and they both were huddled over wrapping their arms around their bodies. The cold bit through me as if I had stepped into a frozen lake, making me shiver and my teeth chatter. We had gone through some pretty weird stuff and I didn't want to give up now but I felt that every ounce of energy was being sapped out of my body, and that just as I thought I could go no further, we stumbled upon a narrow passageway hidden behind a veil of shimmering mist. It was as if the very fabric of reality had been torn asunder, revealing a glimpse of the unknown beyond.

"This must be the way out," Akira said, her voice filled with relief.

"Let's not waste any time," Talia said, her voice firm, "we need to find our way out before it's too late."

One clue had led to another with no answers and I was tired and my stomach was telling me that it was definitely time to eat as the hunger growl echoed off the walls of the tunnels like a grizzly bear woken from hibernation. I was happy to find the way out quickly. I had started to trust Talia, but as we pressed on I could feel a sense of malevolence and energy watching our every move with unseen eyes.

"We're getting close," Talia said, her voice barely above a whisper.

"To what? I don't have a good feeling about this."

And then, just as suddenly as it had begun, the darkness lifted, revealing a vast chamber bathed in the soft glow of starlight and warmth. At the centre of the chamber stood an empty pedestal, its surface polished to a mirror-like sheen.

"We've made it," I said, relief flooding through me.

But as we approached the pedestal, a sense of unease settled over me, again. Something wasn't right.

"Where is she?" Akira asked, her voice filled with confusion.

I looked around the chamber, searching for any sign of Nemesis, but she was nowhere to be found.

"She's not here," I said, my voice filled with frustration. "Nyx doesn't know where her daughter is."

Talia's face fell, her shoulders slumping in defeat. "Then we're no closer to finding her than we were before at the start of this quest."

But even as despair threatened to overwhelm us, I could feel a glimmer of hope stirring deep within me. We may not have found Nemesis, but we had survived the darkness of the cave, and that in itself was a victory worth celebrating and the gut feeling that she had been there, meant we were on the right tracks, but which one were we meant to take?

"We may not have found her yet," I said, my voice filled with determination, "but we won't give up. We'll keep searching until we find her, no matter what it takes."

With that, we turned and began the long journey back through the caverns, knowing that our quest was far from over. But this time with more determination, and the knowledge of the expectations of the challenges along the way, we knew it wouldn't take as long to get out and back to the surface.

Emerging into the dappled light of the forest once more felt like being reborn. The air, fresh and filled with the scent of pine and earth, was a welcome change from the musty, oppressive atmosphere of the cave. We paused at the cave entrance, taking a moment to breathe deeply and savour the sunlight filtering through the trees.

"We'll regroup back at camp," Talia said, her voice carrying a note of renewed resolve, "we need to reassess our strategy and figure out our next move."

The journey back to our campsite was uneventful, once we passed through the thorny path, the forest trail was familiar with its natural beauty. Birds sang overhead, and the rustling of leaves created a soothing backdrop to our thoughts. I found myself reflecting on our adventure in the cave, the challenges we had faced, and the mysterious energies we had encountered.

As we approached the makeshift camp, I noticed something different. The clearing where we had set up our tents seemed to shimmer with a faint, otherworldly light. I exchanged a curious glance with Akira, who nodded, confirming that she saw it too.

Talia, however, was unfazed. "It's a protective enchantment," she explained, catching our puzzled expressions, "the forest spirits are watching over us. They know we mean no harm."

That night, as we settled around the campfire, Talia had gathered some wild hazelnuts, pine nuts and chestnuts and even though I would have preferred a double cheeseburger my stomach stopped sounding its disapproving objection to not having eaten. We shared our thoughts, discussing possible locations where Nemesis might be hiding and how we could navigate the challenges ahead. Talia's leadership was unwavering, her confidence in our mission a beacon of strength for all of us.

As the fire crackled and the stars began to emerge in the sky above, I felt a sense of camaraderie and purpose binding us together. We were not just three individuals on a quest; we were a family, united by a common goal and driven by an unyielding determination and the dangers we had overcome together.

"We'll need to explore other parts of the forest," Talia said, her voice steady. "Nyx's influence is strong, but there are other forces at play. We must be prepared for anything."

Akira nodded, her eyes reflecting the firelight. "We've come this far, we can't turn back now."

I agreed, feeling a surge of resolve. "No matter what lies ahead, we'll face it together."

As the night deepened, we retired to our tent, each of us lost in our thoughts. Sleep came quickly, filled with dreams of dark caves, shimmering pools of moonlight, and the enigmatic presence of Nemesis. I awoke several times, the silence of the forest both comforting and unsettling, a reminder of the mystical forces that surrounded us.

- Chapter 14 -

The Strange Lady

I awoke first that morning, to rain. Great! Just what we needed.

"Oliver?" I turned to see Akira sitting up rubbing her eyes.

"Yes?"

"Maybe we should go back to camp, the actual one," she said, "they may be able to help us, besides what if they already found her?"

"You have a point, but we should ask Talia, it is her mother. She knows more about the camp anyway, I already forgot where it is."

We waited for Talia to wake up and I told her what Akira told me.

"If we go back to camp we can actually sleep, on beds, eat whatever we want."

"And change our clothes," Akira put in, "and shower." I rolled my eyes, I kind of enjoyed not having to shower and changing my clothes.

She looked at us, "I guess, be warned though people may treat you differently."

"What do you mean?" Akira asked.

"If Nemesis hasn't been found and we don't have her, people may treat us differently, they will treat us like failures."

"But we went on a quest they didn't, they were scared, they didn't even try."

"That doesn't matter."

We all thought about the best option, stay and look or go back to camp?

"Camp," we all agreed.

"We will go back to camp with the information we have, shower, eat and replenish our stocks, clean clothes, extra batteries and proper food other than beef jerky," I said, smiling. "Then we can continue with the quest."

The journey back to the main camp was slow and arduous. The rain had turned the forest paths into a muddy mess, making each step a slippery challenge. As we approached the edge of Epping Forest, a sense of urgency quickened our pace. We were all eager for the comforts of camp but also wary of the reception we might receive. Talia's words about being treated as failures weighed heavily on our minds.

Suddenly, Akira stopped in her tracks, her eyes fixed on something in the distance. "Did you see that?" she whispered, pointing towards a large rock partially obscured by dense foliage.

We all turned to look. At first, there was nothing, just the steady fall of rain and the quiet whisper of the forest. Then, as the wind shifted the branches, we saw her.

A young woman, barely looking twenty years old, was crouched behind the rock. Her long black hair was matted with dirt, and her deep brown eyes, nearly black, were wide with fear or perhaps something else entirely. She looked out of place in this wilderness, her presence both a mystery and unusual.

"Who is she?" I asked, my voice low and suspicious.

Talia stepped forward cautiously. "We should find out."

We approached slowly, not wanting to startle her. The woman's eyes darted between us, her body tense and ready to flee. Talia raised her hands in a gesture of peace.

"Hey there," Talia said softly, "are you okay? Do you need help?"

The woman didn't respond immediately. Her gaze lingered on Talia for much longer than felt normal, her expression a mix of recognition and something deeper. Finally, she seemed to relax just a fraction, though her eyes remained wary.

"What's your name?" I asked, trying to sound as gentle as possible despite my distrust.

For a moment, it seemed she wouldn't answer. But then, in a voice barely above a whisper, she said, "Justice."

There was something about the way she said it that sent a shiver down my spine. It felt familiar, like a name whispered in a dream. Talia's eyes widened slightly, a flicker of recognition passing over her face, but she quickly masked it.

"Do you have somewhere to go? Someone to be with?" Talia asked, concern colouring her voice.

Justice shook her head slowly, her eyes still locked on Talia.

"Why are you here?" I asked, unable to keep the suspicion from my voice. "This isn't a place for wandering alone."

Justice's eyes finally broke away from Talia to meet mine. There was something unsettling and macabre in her gaze, something that made my skin crawl with unease. "I am here because I choose to be. My reasons are my own."

Her answer was cryptic, and it did nothing to ease my mistrust. "We should get moving," I said, not taking my eyes off her. "The rain isn't going to let up, and we need to get back to camp."

Talia hesitated, glancing between Justice and the direction of the camp. "You can come with us if you want. We have food and shelter."

Justice considered this for a long moment before nodding slowly. "Thank you."

As we set off, I kept a close eye on her. There was something about her that I couldn't shake, a sense of unease that clung to her like the mud on her clothes. She stayed close to Talia, her eyes often drifting back to her as if drawn by some invisible force.

The journey back was quiet, the only sounds were the rain and our footsteps squelching through the mud. The forest seemed to close in around us, the trees whispering secrets that only Justice seemed to understand. I couldn't help but wonder who she really was and why she seemed so fixated on Talia.

"We need to find a place to rest," Talia said after a while, her eyes scanning the forest, "this rain is getting worse."

We found a small clearing sheltered by a large overhanging rock. It wasn't much, but it offered some protection from the weather. We set up a makeshift camp, using what little dry wood we could find to start a fire.

As we huddled around the flickering flames, the atmosphere was tense. Justice sat slightly apart from the group, her eyes never straying far from Talia. I couldn't shake the feeling that there was more to her than met the eye, something she was keeping hidden.

"Tell us about yourself, Justice," Akira said, breaking the silence. "Where are you from?"

Justice looked into the fire, her expression unreadable. "I come from a place far from here, a place of balance and justice." Her answer was vague, and it did nothing to ease my suspicions.

"Why are you here?" I pressed. "What do you want?"

Her eyes met mine, and for a moment, there was a flicker of something - sadness, maybe? "I am here because I have a duty."

Her cryptic responses only deepened my mistrust. Justice's gaze shifted to Talia, and for a moment, there was a look of profound sadness in her eyes. "I cannot say more. Not yet."

The day wore on, and despite the tension, exhaustion eventually claimed us. We took turns keeping watch, the rain a constant, soothing presence as it drummed against the rock above us.

As dawn approached, the rain finally began to let up, and the first rays of sunlight pierced through the canopy. We packed up our camp, ready to continue our journey.

"Justice, you're welcome to stay with us," Akira said, her voice kind but firm, "but if you're hiding something, we need to know. We need to trust each other."

Justice nodded, her eyes filled with a mixture of gratitude and sorrow. "I understand. I will tell you what I can, when the time is right."

As we set off again after the rain stopped, the forest seemed to come alive with the promise of maybe finding Nemesis at Olympus. The tension from the night before lingered, but there was also a sense of hope. We were on the right path, and though the journey ahead was uncertain, we faced it together. We had already defeated Medusa and the Graeae, the river Lethe not including all the other hardships and challenges, so what else could possibly be worse? After we would get to camp, sleep and eat we would be ready to face anything and as we walked, I kept a close watch on Justice, determined to uncover her secrets and protect my friends. For in this forest of shadows and whispers, trust was the most valuable commodity of all.

As the sun climbed higher in the sky, we trudged onward. The air was heavy with the scent of damp earth and wet leaves. Every now and then, I'd catch Justice stealing glances at Talia, her expression a mixture of sorrow and longing.

We stopped for a brief rest, and it was then that Talia finally spoke up. "Justice, why do you keep looking at me like that?"

Justice's gaze locked onto Talia, and for a moment, it seemed like she might not answer. Then she sighed, the weight of years in her voice. "Talia, there's something you need to know."

The forest seemed to hold its breath as we all turned to look at her, a sense of anticipation hanging heavy in the air. Even the birdsong seemed to fade into the background, as if waiting for what was to come.

"Talia, I am... I am your mother. I am Nemesis."

The words hung in the air like a thunderclap, reverberating through the clearing. Talia's eyes went wide with shock, her breath catching in her throat. She stared at the woman standing before her, her mind obviously struggling to process the revelation.

My heart pounded in my chest as I watched the scene unfold, the truth hitting us like a tidal wave.

The tension was palpable, each of us frozen in place as we waited for Talia's response.

"You?" Talia finally managed to say, her voice barely above a whisper. "You're my mother?"

Justice nodded slowly, tears glistening in her eyes. "Yes, Talia. I am."

Talia's reaction was immediate and visceral. She took a step back, her face a mask of hurt and anger. "You were supposed to come for me when I was six, you never showed up. You abandoned me."

Justice reached out a hand, but Talia recoiled, her eyes blazing with betrayal. "I had my reasons," she began, but Talia cut her off with a sharp gesture.

"Save it," Talia snapped, "I don't want to hear your excuses."

Justice's face crumpled, and she lowered her hand, her expression one of deep sorrow.

She glanced at Talia's face, her eyes narrowing in confusion. "Talia, why do you smile like that, my child?"

Talia's permanent smile hardened which was a shame, the days beforehand it had started to soften, as if she was getting more comfortable but as soon as Nemesis said that, Talias guard seemed to go back up. "It's none of your concern."

Akira and I stood in stunned silence, unsure of what to say or do. The truth had come out, but it had brought more pain than resolution.

As we continued our journey, the tension between Talia and Justice was transparent. Talia kept her distance, her body language stiff and closed off. Justice's eyes never left her daughter, a permanent, sad smile on her lips, but she didn't comment further.

Akira stayed close to Talia, offering silent support, whilst I was walking behind Justice to make sure she wouldn't run away. We had bound her hands with the little rope we had to ensure she wouldn't run away, though I didn't think she would. I could see the turmoil in Talia's eyes, the conflict between the need for answers and the pain of betrayal. It was a lot to process, and I could only hope that in time, she would find a way to make peace with it all.

For now, we had a journey to complete, and as much as Talia's world had been turned upside down, we needed to stay focused. Nemesis, or Justice, I wasn't sure what to call her, had revealed her true identity, but her reasons for being here remained a mystery. And until we knew more, trust would remain elusive in this forest full of secrets.

It felt as if the trees were whispering mysteries and secrets that only Nemesis seemed to understand. I couldn't shake the feeling that she held the key to something greater, something that had brought her to us.

The sun climbed higher in the sky, casting dappled shadows on the forest floor. Talia walked with her head held high, her jaw set in determination. Despite the pain of Nemesis's revelation, she refused to let it break her. She was a daughter of Olympus, strong and resilient, and she would not be defined by the actions of her mother.

As we walked, I found myself drawn to Nemesis, the woman who had upended our world with a single confession. There was a darkness in her eyes, a heaviness that spoke of a lifetime of regret.

I wondered what had led her to this moment, what secrets lay buried beneath her stoic facade.

"Are you okay?" I asked, falling into step beside her. I still didn't trust her, especially now we had actually found her. But it would be rude to not ask a Goddess right?

Nemesis glanced at me, her eyes unreadable. "I'm fine," she said softly, though her voice held a hint of weariness.

I didn't press further, sensing that she wasn't ready to share more. Instead, we walked in silence, each lost in our own thoughts as the forest enveloped us in its embrace.

Hours passed, the sun tracing its arc across the sky as we journeyed into the heart of the woods, we tied Nemesis's arms behind her back, in case she did try to run away it would be very difficult to keep her balance, though we doubted she would try. The air grew thick with humidity, the scent of wet earth mingling with the tang of greenery. Sweat trickled down my spine, but still we pressed on, powered by the belief or naivety of the presumption that we would finally get answers.

As we walked, I couldn't shake the feeling of being watched, of unseen eyes following our every move. I glanced over my shoulder, but there was nothing there, just the endless expanse of trees stretching out behind us.

"We should take a break," Talia said, her voice breaking through the stillness of the forest. "We've been walking for hours."

I nodded, grateful for the chance to rest my weary legs. We found a clearing bathed in dappled sunlight and sank to the ground, our backs against the rough bark of towering Scots pine trees. The aroma from the resin from the trees was sweet and piney, the smell of christmas, giving me a sense of calm after our long weary walk.

"We need to talk..." Talia said, breaking the silence. Her voice was steady, but I could see the turmoil in her eyes, "...About Nemesis."

I glanced at Nemesis, who sat apart from the group, her expression unreadable. She seemed lost in thought, a distant look in her eyes as if she were seeing something beyond the reach of mortal vision.

"What do you want to know?" I asked, turning back to Talia.

Talia hesitated, her gaze flickering between Nemesis and me. "I don't know," she admitted. "I just... I need to understand, why she left, what she wants."

I nodded, understanding her need for answers. We all did. But I knew that uncovering Nemesis's secrets would not be easy, that there were depths to her darkness that we had yet to fathom.

"What do we do with her?" Akira asked, "Do we go back to camp?"

I shrugged my shoulders.

"No, we need to go to Olympus," Talia said quietly.

"Isn't that in Greece?"

"It changes, gods need a place to lay low."

"Oh... alright then," I said, how can you just change it, does the castle teleport or do you build a whole new one?

"It's somewhere here in London," she reached

into her jeans pocket and pulled out a piece of paper with small writing on it, "these are the places it has been over the last few years."

I looked at the piece of paper: India, Australia, The Maldives. I looked at the most recent one: London, Big Ben.

As we sat in the clearing, the afternoon sun casting long shadows through the trees, the reality of our situation began to sink in. Nemesis, the goddess of retribution and balance, was Talia's mother. The revelation had sent shockwaves through our group, and now we had to figure out what to do next.

Talia stared at the ground, her face a mask of conflicting emotions. "We need to go to Olympus," she repeated, her voice firmer this time. "If anyone can give us answers, it's the gods."

Akira frowned. "But what about camp? Shouldn't we go back and regroup, get more supplies, maybe even some help?"

I shook my head. "Going back to camp might delay us too much. We need to stay focused on the goal. Olympus is our best bet."

Nemesis, still bound and sitting slightly apart from us, watched the exchange with a calm, almost resigned expression. She hadn't said much since her revelation, and I couldn't tell if she was relieved or regretful about finally revealing her identity to Talia.

"Uh- Talia," I said and she looked back at me, "do you want to talk to her now, privately?"

"No, it's fine," she replied, "answers will have to wait, I've waited a long time for this, a few more days won't hurt."

Talia stood up, brushing dirt off her trousers. "Alright, we head to Olympus but first, we need to get out of these woods. Epping Forest is like a labyrinth, and we can't afford to get lost."

We gathered our things and set off again, the trees towering above us like ancient sentinels. The forest seemed endless, each path looking identical to the last, and it wasn't long before we began to feel the toll of our journey had had upon us so far.

As we walked, the tension between Talia and Nemesis was undeniable, both wanting to tell a story but both scared of the truth. Nemesis stayed silent, her gaze often fixed on the ground, while Talia's face was a storm of emotions. I could tell she was struggling to reconcile the image of her mother as a goddess with the abandonment she had felt all her life.

"Why did you come back now?" Talia asked abruptly, not looking at Nemesis.

Nemesis hesitated, her eyes flickering with a mix of pain and determination. "I came back because I had to. There's something happening, something that threatens all of us. The gods are in danger, and so is humanity."

Talia's brow furrowed. "What do you mean? What's happening?"

Nemesis sighed, a deep, weary sound. "I can't explain everything now. But there's a force rising, something that could bring about the end of both the mortal and divine worlds. I came back to find you, to protect you and your brother."

Talia scoffed. "Protect me? After all this time? You think you can just waltz back into my life and play the protective mother?"

Nemesis's eyes were filled with sorrow. "I know I've hurt you, Talia. And I don't expect you to forgive me. But I promise you, I had my reasons. Zeus... he's part of why I left."

Talia's eyes narrowed. "Zeus? What about him?"

I looked at Nemesis, what had my father done, I read the legends, I knew he wasn't the nicest person, known to have anger issues, hence thunderstorms and lightning bolts and all of that, but he seriously didn't seem as if he would destroy the world, Zeus, King of the gods... my dad?

Nemesis opened her mouth to answer, but Talia cut her off. "No, never mind, I don't want to hear it. Whatever excuses you have, keep them to yourself. We need to focus on getting out of here and reaching Olympus."

Nemesis' pupils got smaller and she started shaking. "Talia, please not Olympus," she begged.

Talia looked at her mother, I could tell she was confused, she evidently loved her mother, she had risked her life to come find her, but here she was staring her down, whilst her mum was on the floor begging.

It was quite clear Talia wasn't going to give in, Nemesis knew it, I knew it, Akira knew it. Nemesis turned around and grabbed my legs.

"Uh..."

"Please, Oliver, please."

Was it rude to shake a Goddess off my leg? Because that's what I did.

- Chapter 15 -

Olympus and Big Ben

The tension created by Nemesis's revelations had only complicated matters. We trudged onward, the canopy of trees above casting dappled shadows on the forest floor.

"Talia, please, you have to understand," Nemesis began again as we pushed through a dense thicket, "I'm here to protect you. Olympus is not safe. There are things you don't know, things that I need to explain."

Talia spun around, her face a mask of anger and frustration. "I don't want to hear it, Nemesis. You had your chance to explain, and you chose to leave me instead. Whatever danger there is, we'll face it together, without you."

Nemesis's eyes filled with tears, and she sank to her knees in the muddy path. "Please, Talia, you don't know what Zeus is capable of. I had to run to keep you safe."

I stepped forward, gently pulling Talia away from her mother. "We don't have time for this. We need to keep moving."

As we continued our journey, Nemesis's desperate pleas echoed behind us, a haunting reminder of the rift between mother and daughter. Despite her protests, we pressed on, determined to reach Olympus.

Hours passed, and the forest began to thin. The air grew cooler, and the sounds of the city began to infiltrate the quiet of the woodland. We were nearing the edge of Epping Forest, a quick train journey into the centre of London to get to Olympus, a surreal thought that we were on our way to the home of the gods.

Nemesis continued to beg, her voice raw with emotion. "Please, Talia, don't go to Olympus. There's more at stake than you realise."

Talia's face was set in stone, her eyes forward, ignoring her mother's pleas. Akira and I exchanged worried glances, but we knew better than to intervene. This was Talia's fight, and she needed to see it through.

We emerged from the underground station into

the bustling streets of London. The silhouette of Big Ben towering above us filled me with a renewed sense of purpose. We were close now, so close to the answers we sought.

As we approached the iconic landmark, Nemesis made one last attempt to stop us. "Talia, I beg you. Listen to me. Zeus will stop at nothing to protect his secrets. If you go to Olympus, you might not come back."

Talia turned to face her mother, her eyes blazing with determination. "I've spent my whole life wondering why you left, why you abandoned me. Now I have the chance to find the truth, and nothing you say will stop me." She paused, taking a deep breath to steady herself. "You can either come with us and face whatever is up there, or stay behind but I'm going."

Nemesis sighed and started walking behind Talia. I understood where Talia was coming from, her mother had left her, yet I felt bad for Nemesis not even being able to explain herself. I felt as if there was more to this than a mother trying to find excuses for her mistakes, it felt like desperation of a mum trying to keep her child safe. I looked at Akira and I knew she was thinking the same.

Big Ben loomed above us, its massive clock face a guard watching over the city. We approached the entrance, the air heavy with anticipation. The iconic landmark was more than just a tourist attraction, it was the gateway to Olympus.

Entering the clock tower, we had paid and entered as tourists in an attempt to not bring attention to ourselves, the interior was a stark contrast to its grand exterior. The walls were lined with intricate carvings and ancient symbols, pulsating with a faint, otherworldly glow.

The air hummed with energy, a tangible reminder that this place was more than it seemed.

We climbed the narrow spiral staircase, each step bringing us closer to the heart of the tower and the secrets it held.

We walked up the stairs, even though we had to stop a few times.

"Why are there so many stairs?" Akira panted.

Nemesis was the only one who seemed to be refreshed, no sweat and no heavy breathing.

Even Talia seemed to get tired, we were about halfway up when we saw a few other people. Tourists probably, a woman with light brown hair, a buff man with a black beard, a young girl who looked about seven and a baby.

"Howdy," said the woman in a thick Texan accent, eyeing us.

"Hi," Talia said and Akira smiled.

I didn't say anything.

"Why is your mum tied up?"

"Uh- we're actors, part of the scene."

"Where are the camera's?" asked the young girl.

"Penny," warned the woman.

"They are coming in a little while, just helps to get into character first."

"Oh well, you look very nice, good luck."

"Thank you," Akira smiled, trying to suppress a laugh.

"Anyway, I'm Lara," the woman introduced herself with a warm smile, extending a hand despite the odd circumstances. The bearded man nodded in acknowledgment, keeping a protective hand on the shoulder of the young girl, Penny, who looked at us with her wide, brown, curious eyes. The baby in a sling on Lara's chest gurgled, blissfully unaware of the tension around them.

"I'm Akira, and this is Talia and Oliver," Akira responded, shaking Lara's hand, "...and our mother, Justice," she said in a friendly tone.

"It's nice to meet you," Lara said, her gaze flicking between Nemesis and the rest of us. "Why are you guys filming at big ben?"

"We're, uh, on a bit of an adventure," Talia replied, trying to sound casual, but it wasn't working very well. "Just seeing the sights."

"Why are you carrying swords?" Penny asked.

"We uh- bought them from a gift shop, makes it feel the part."

Lara's eyes lingered on Nemesis's bound hands, a flicker of suspicion crossing her face. "An adventure, huh? Well, be careful. This place can be a bit tricky to navigate. Especially without a camera crew."

"We'll manage," I said tersely, eager to end the conversation and continue our ascent. "Thank you for the advice."

I pulled aside Talia and Akira, "I think we need to move quicker before someone else gets suspicious and calls security, it's not everyday you see someone tied up."

As we continued up the staircase, the family fell behind, their voices fading into the background. I couldn't help but feel a sense of relief. We didn't need more complications, or distractions.

The higher we climbed, the more the air seemed to hum with an ethereal energy. It was as if the very walls of Big Ben were alive, vibrating with the power of Olympus. Each step brought us closer to our destination, and the anticipation was almost unbearable, Talia kept twiddling with her fingers and Akira was running her fingers through her hair.

As we reached the top, the colossal clock face came into view. The massive gears and cogs interlocked in a precise dance, their rhythmic ticking echoing through the chamber. The light streaming in from the clock's face cast an majestic glow on the surroundings, adding to the sense of wonder and anticipation.

"Now all we have to do is find the entrance," I said, "Talia?"

"Sorry," she said, "I don't know where it is."

Akira started looking around, "Do you know what it looks like?"

"A door, probably but not somewhere too obvious, I don't think they would want ordinary people going to Olympus."

I started looking, but kept banging my head on metal rods. I looked at Nemesis, she had to know where it was.

"Talia," Nemesis said softly, breaking the silence. "I know you don't trust me, and you have every right not to. But I promise, I am here to protect you. Zeus... he has secrets that could destroy us all."

Talia turned to face her, her expression hard. "And why should I believe you? After everything?"

Nemesis looked down, her eyes filled with regret. "Because I never stopped loving you. I did what I did to keep you safe. To keep you hidden from those who would use you." She eyed us suspiciously.

Despite Nemesis's desperate plea, Talia remained unmoved, her distrust of her mother obvious in the tense air of the clock tower. Akira and I exchanged uncertain glances, unsure of how to navigate the strained dynamic between mother and daughter. Nemesis's revelation had brought us to the heart of London, to Big Ben itself, but the door to Olympus remained elusive.

"We need to find that door," I muttered, frustration mounting as we searched the chamber. The clock's gears loomed large around us, their intricate mechanisms a striking vision of intricacies and engineering, however we had to move on with the quest and finding the opening to Olympus, Nemesis must have known where the door lay.

"Nemesis, you must know where it is."

Nemesis closed her eyes briefly, her face a mask of sorrow. "I do know," she admitted quietly, her voice barely audible over the ticking of the clock. "But I cannot simply reveal it. There are rules, ancient protections that even I must obey."

Talia clenched her fists, her resolve hardening. "Then tell us how to find it," she demanded, her voice cutting through the tension.

Nemesis hesitated, weighing her words carefully. "There is a riddle," she began, her gaze shifting to the towering clock face. "A puzzle that guards the entrance to Olympus. It changes with each passing hour, a testament to the ever-shifting nature of the gods."

"A riddle?" Akira echoed, her brow furrowing in confusion. "What kind of riddle?"

Nemesis sighed, her eyes distant as if recalling a distant memory. "It is said that only those who understand the balance of power and humility can unlock the door," she explained cryptically.

"But the answer lies not in words, but in actions."

Talia exchanged a wary glance with Akira and me. "Actions?" she repeated, scepticism evident in her voice.

Nemesis nodded solemnly. "Yes, you must prove yourselves worthy," she said, her gaze lingering on Talia, "each challenge faced with courage, each test met with humility. Only then will the way to Olympus be revealed."

"We don't have time for games," I interjected, frustration colouring my tone. "If you know where it is, just show us."

Nemesis shook her head, her expression pained. "I cannot," she insisted.

"Why not, you owe us?" Akira asked.

Nemesis laughed, "Owe you? I owe you nothing Akira."

"But you owe me," Talia said, "you left me."

I could see the colour drain from Nemesis's face.

"I will, if you stop smiling like that, you have such a pretty face, why spoil it with such a fake smile?"

I could see Talia getting angrier, "You are in no place to bargain with me," she said.

Nemesis sighed, "Very well," she walked over to Talia and whispered in her ear, I didn't understand why, she would tell us anyway.

"So you lied? There's no riddle?"

"Talia, you don't understand, please I'll do anything just don't go to Olympus."

"I'm sorry mother, but we need to do this," Talia said.

Talia started to walk towards the clock, right under the three there was a faint shimmer.

Akira and I started walking towards it with Nemesis following behind us.

"Can you give me a boost?" she asked Akira. She hopped onto Akira's shoulders and opened the small door and crawled through.

"Okay Nemesis, you're next."

"I can't go with you," she said, in a soft voice.

I rolled my eyes and looked at Akira, why were goddesses so difficult?

Akira tried to lift Nemesis, then immediately dropped her.

"I thought goddesses would be light," she said.

Nemesis gasped, "How rude! How dare you!"

"Just go in," I was starting to get really irritated.

"I told you I can't!"

"Just do it!"

After ages of lifting, running and moaning we finally managed to haul her in. Akira went in next. I was relieved but then I heard her. "Seriously?"

"What?" I called, she didn't sound as if she was in trouble, just annoyed.

"She's not moving,"

I sighed, "Just push her."

"Oliver, she's a goddess, I can't just do that," her voice echoed.

"Oh, so now you recognise that I'm a goddess?"

"Just get me up there," Akira's hand dangled down from the small ornate door and lifted me up. I saw Nemesis sitting there, her head touching the small white passageway with her legs and arms folded.

Akira tried to crawl in front of her but wasn't able to. I managed to sneak past her without her seeing me from behind and dragged her by her hair, I didn't care if she was a goddess, I didn't care if she was the king, I didn't care if she was the lord high empress of the universe, she was a royal pain in the butt.

- Chapter 16 -

Zeus and a Row

The vastness of Olympus unfurled before us as we stepped through the threshold of Big Ben. The transition from bustling London to the realm of the gods was seamless yet profound. The air crackled with a sense of ancient power and mystery, reminding us that we were entering a domain untouched by mortal hands, a parallel universe.

Olympus greeted us with its timeless splendour. The architecture, a blend of classical Greek grandeur and celestial craftsmanship, captivated our senses. Marble columns rose majestically, adorned with intricate carvings that told stories of myth and legend. Soft, ambient light bathed the surroundings, emanating from luminous orbs that hovered serenely overhead, casting ethereal shadows upon the polished marble floors.

Celestial gardens sprawled in vibrant hues unseen on Earth. Flowers of every colour swayed in a gentle breeze, their fragrances blending harmoniously with the faint scent of ambrosia. Trees with silvered leaves whispered ancient wisdom, their branches reaching towards the heavens in silent reverence.

The atmosphere, while peaceful, carried an undercurrent of power-reminder that Olympus was the realm where gods ruled over both mortals and immortals alike.

Guided by unseen forces, we traversed the celestial gardens, following a path that seemed to lead inevitably towards the heart of Olympus.

Finally, we arrived at the Throne Room. Twelve thrones of pure gold gleamed in a semicircle at the far end, each intricately adorned with symbols representing the gods they belonged to. The room itself expanded infinitely, its domed ceiling adorned with constellations that shimmered like real stars in the heavens.

As we stood before the thrones in reverent awe, our attention was drawn to the figure seated upon Zeus's throne, the ruler of Olympus himself, Zeus.

His presence commanded both respect and apprehension, his gaze piercing through the depths of our beings.

Zeus appeared as a formidable figure, embodying the regal authority befitting the king of gods. His physique was imposing yet graceful, his stature towering over the other gods. Long, flowing robes of shimmering white draped his form, adorned with motifs of thunderbolts and storm clouds that seemed to shift and flicker with the faintest movements. A crown of golden laurel leaves encircled his head, symbolising victory and rulership. His hair, a cascade of silver-white curls, framed a handsome face yet bore the weight of ages - eyes as deep as the night sky, filled with both wisdom and an undeniable spark of mischief. A beard, meticulously groomed and as white as fresh snow, flowed down to his chest.

Upon his outstretched arm rested a sceptre of pure gold, topped with a glowing orb that pulsed with a celestial light - a symbol of his dominion over the heavens and the earth.

With every movement, the air around Zeus seemed to crackle with latent energy, a testament to the potent power that lay dormant within him.

"Nemesis," Zeus said, his voice softer now as he turned to face her. "You left Olympus without a word. Why?"

Nemesis squared her shoulders, meeting Zeus's gaze with unflinching resolve. "Because of you," she said quietly, "because of what you became."

Zeus's expression darkened, a storm brewing in his eyes. "Explain," he demanded, his voice a low growl.

"Nemesis," Talia spoke up, stepping forward to stand beside her mother. "What do you mean? What happened between you and Zeus?"

Nemesis hesitated, her eyes flickering with a mixture of pain and determination. "Zeus," she began, her voice steady despite the emotions roiling within her. "He... he desired me. When I refused him, he became enraged."

Silence descended upon the chamber, broken only by the crackle of distant thunder. Zeus's face was a mask of conflicting emotions, his hands tightening into fists on the armrests of his throne.

"You dare accuse me?" Zeus thundered, his voice shaking the very foundations of Olympus.

Lightning crackled around him, a testament to his growing fury.

"Nemesis, is this true?" Talia asked, turning to her mother with wide eyes. Nemesis hesitated, her gaze locked with Zeus's.

"Yes," she said finally, her voice barely a whisper, "it's true."

"But that still doesn't explain why you never came for me all those years ago."

"Listen Talia, you can't live among gods for more than a few months, if I took you with me, you wouldn't of made it and I had duties to attend to"

Talia stepped forward, in front of her mother, her smile a mask of conflicting emotions. "You hurt my mother," she said, her voice trembling with anger. "You drove her away."

Zeus's eyes narrowed, his gaze flickering between us. "She betrayed me, she defied me."

"She is my mother," Talia shot back, her voice rising, "and you may be King of the Gods. But you have no right to hurt her."

Zeus's expression hardened, his voice cold as ice. "She is a goddess of retribution, Talia. She brings justice to those who deserve it."

"She is also my mother," Talia insisted, her eyes blazing with defiance, "and you will not harm her."

Zeus's lips curled into a cruel smile. "Bring her to me, boy," he said, turning to me with a dismissive gesture, "I will make her see reason."

I stepped forward, my heart pounding in my chest. This was Zeus, King of the gods, my father. The man I had never known but had always wanted to impress, I looked at Akira who looked like she was going to throw up, I didn't know what to do, impress my father who I had longed to meet for all these years or protect the one person who might consider me a friend.

"We will not let you hurt her," I said, my voice steady despite my fear, "she is our companion, our friend." Maybe, if she wanted to be my friend, I didn't care. "And she deserves better than your anger."

Zeus's eyes narrowed, his gaze locked with mine. "You dare defy me, mortal?"

"I dare protect my friends," I said, my voice echoing through the chamber, "even if it means standing up to you."

Zeus's fury was incontrovertible, his hands crackling with lightning. "You will regret this, boy," he said, his voice low and dangerous. "I am Zeus, King of the Gods."

"And I am Oliver," I replied, my voice unwavering. "Son of Zeus, well you, I guess. And I will not let you harm my friends."

The tension in the chamber was thick, a storm of emotions and power swirling around us. Talia stood beside me, her jaw set in determination.

Akira hovered close, her eyes flickering with worry.

"You are a fool, boy," Zeus said finally, his voice cold, "but you have courage. I will give you that."

He turned to Akira, his gaze softening, "Well, what about you my dear daughter. Will you do what is right?" he glared at me.

"Yes, I shall," Akira said, moving closer to us, taking the sword from me and pulling it out of the case, "I may not know how to fight, I may not know advanced calculus, but I do know what is right." She lifted the sword, then promptly threw up. But I was proud nonetheless.

"Alright then," Zeus said, "if that's what you desire," he opened his palm and released millions of tiny thunderbolts.

Great! just what we needed, another fight. With my dad, no less, that was just how I pictured meeting him, definitely not hugging or sharing stories whilst we all hugged and vowed to never let go. We shouldn't have imagined anything else with a god as a father, at least I found out where I get my short temper from. we had already faced a sculptor and three old ladies, how hard was a dad with power that unrivalled anything on earth.

Zeus's fury erupted into a tempest of divine power, the very air crackling with lightning as he unleashed his wrath upon us. The Throne Room of Olympus trembled under the onslaught of his thunderbolts, each strike lighting up the vast expanse like a wrathful symphony of light and sound. The celestial gardens outside shuddered as if in sympathy, their tranquillity shattered by the chaos within.

As the onslaught intensified, Talia and Akira stood firm beside me, their resolve unyielding despite the overwhelming power of the king of gods. Talia's eyes blazed with defiance, her stance unwavering as she shielded her mother, Nemesis, from Zeus's wrath. Akira, though visibly shaken, stood firm and gripped my sword with determination, ready to defend us against our own father's fury.

I faced Zeus, my own father, with a mixture of fear and determination. His gaze bore into me, a storm of emotions raging within those ancient eyes. This was not the reunion I had imagined, a clash of wills and principles rather than a moment of familial embrace. Yet, in that tumultuous chamber, I found a strength I never knew I possessed.

"Stop this, Father!" I shouted above the thunderous din, my voice trembling but resolute. "This isn't the way!"

Zeus's eyes narrowed, his thunderous voice echoing through the chamber. "You dare challenge me, boy? You dare stand against your own blood?"

"I mean, yeah, kind of," I could hear Akira slapping her face, but what was I meant to say, I hadn't practised this.

"Ah! The arrogance of mortals, you think you can stand against me?"

I squared my shoulders, summoning whatever bravado I could muster. "Well, yeah," I shot back, my voice tinged with fear and determination. "I mean, this whole lightning show isn't exactly a warm family reunion, Dad."

The corners of Zeus's lips twitched, momentarily caught off guard by my retort. The tension in the room eased for a brief moment as gods and mortals exchanged bewildered glances. Even Talia couldn't help but smirk faintly at my unexpected sass in the face of divine wrath.

Zeus's expression hardened once more, but I detected a trace of reluctant admiration gleaming in his stormy eyes.

"You have your mother's spirit, boy," he rumbled, the tempest around him momentarily subsiding. "Very well, let us settle this."

He snapped his fingers and produced a huge lightning bolt. He glared at us, looking for his victim as if he wanted to make an example out of one of us. His eyes zeroed in on Talia, and before any of us could react, he hurled the bolt straight at her.

Talia moved to dodge, but Zeus's aim was impeccable. The lightning bolt struck her shoulder with a blinding flash and a deafening crack. Talia's scream of pain echoed through the chamber as she crumpled to the floor, her body trembling from the shock and her mother rushing to her side in an instant. Yet, even in agony, the strange, permanent smile on her face remained, an eerie contrast to the scene.

"No!" I shouted, rushing to her side. I could feel the electricity still dancing on her skin, but I didn't care, she was my friend, the only person who even bothered to try and get to know me. "Talia, hang on!"

Akira, shaking off her fear, positioned herself between Zeus and Talia, my sword raised with trembling hands. "You've done enough, Father," she declared, her voice surprisingly firm, "leave her alone!"

Before Zeus could unleash another torrent of divine wrath, a new presence entered the Throne Room. Hera, Queen of the Gods, swept in with an aura of authority tempered by an unexpected warmth. Her regal demeanour softened as she approached, her gaze assessing the scene with a mix of concern and resolve.

"Zeus," she said, her voice commanding yet surprisingly gentle, "what is the meaning of this?"

Zeus turned to face his wife, his expression a tumultuous blend of defiance and begrudging respect. "These mortals dare to defy me, Hera," he replied, his voice tinged with lingering anger. "They have no place here."

Hera's eyes flickered with understanding as she glanced at Talia, still prone on the marble floor. "And yet, they stand before you, challenging your authority," she observed, her tone soft yet unwavering.

"They do not belong," Zeus insisted, his voice resonating through the chamber.

Hera approached Talia and knelt beside her, her touch gentle as she assessed the extent of her injuries. Talia's smile remained fixed, but there was a glimmer of gratitude in her eyes.

"These mortals have shown courage and determination," Hera remarked, her voice carrying a note of maternal concern. "Perhaps there is more to them than meets the eye."

Zeus hesitated, his gaze shifting between his wife and the defiant trio before him. The tension in the chamber was palpable, the air thick with unspoken challenges and ancient grievances.

"As Goddess of family," Hera continued, rising to her feet and fixing Zeus with a steady gaze, "it is my decree that they be given a chance to prove themselves."

"Hera, I am the King, I make all the decisions. I rule Olympus."

"And I am your wife, and I've had to put up with plenty of your nonsense over these centuries, what I say goes," she replied coolly, brushing off his retorts.

Zeus's jaw clenched, but he knew better than to defy Hera when she invoked her authority as the Goddess of family. With a reluctant nod, he lowered his arm, the crackling energy dissipating into the ether. Hera seemed to be able to placate him without undermining him, I suppose that in the lyrics of the Eurythmics and Aretha Franklin "Behind every great man there has to be a great woman" is true.

"They may go," Zeus declared gruffly, his voice

carrying the weight of begrudging acceptance.

I exhaled a breath I hadn't realised I'd been holding, relief flooding through me. Akira stepped forward, her sword still at the ready but now lowered in cautious readiness rather than defiance.

"Thank you, Hera," she said, her voice filled with gratitude.

Hera nodded, her expression softening even further. "Remember," she said, her gaze sweeping over us with a hint of a smile, "family is not always blood. Sometimes, it is found in unexpected places."

She turned to leave but stopped and paused for a second, "Nemesis, let's get you cleaned up, then you may return to your mother."

Nemesis disappeared behind one of the golden doors, Hera following suit. Then suddenly Talia's voice broke the silence. "Hera, is my mother going to be safe?"

"Yes, child. Zeus won't harm her again," Hera said with a soft smile.

"Swear it, please."

"I swear it on the Styx, Zeus will not harm your mother"

With those words, she turned and swept out of the Throne Room, her presence fading into the celestial grandeur of Olympus. Zeus watched her go, his expression inscrutable, before he too turned away, leaving us standing amidst the aftermath of our confrontation.

Talia struggled to her feet, supported by Akira and I. Her smile, though still fixed, now held a touch of relief and newfound respect.

"Well," I said, breaking the silence with a nervous chuckle, "that was... intense."

Akira nodded, her gaze still wary but hopeful. "I never thought I'd see the day when Hera intervened on our behalf."

Talia glanced at me, her eyes shimmering with unspoken gratitude. "Thank you," she whispered, her voice carrying the weight of everything left unsaid.

- Chapter 17 -

Going Back to Camp

Leaving Olympus behind was a relief in more ways than one. The journey back to camp felt like a retreat from a battleground where words and wills clashed with the power of gods. Talia walked ahead, her steps measured but with a noticeable droop from where Zeus's lightning had struck her shoulder, though she tried to hide it. Akira stayed close beside her, occasionally glancing back to ensure no lingering traces of Zeus's anger followed us.

The celestial gardens whispered with every breeze that swept through, the flowers shimmering under the fading light of Olympus. It was a more tranquil contrast to the tense atmosphere we had left behind in the Throne Room.

As we walked, I couldn't shake the weight of Zeus's presence or the revelations of my divine heritage. The uncertainty of what lay ahead gnawed at me, but for now, the path to camp offered solace, a return to familiarity amidst the chaos of Olympus.

The air crackled with residual energy, a reminder of Zeus's lingering displeasure. Lightning occasionally danced in the distance, a silent testament to the volatile emotions that governed Olympus.

"We should probably rest," Akira yawned. I could see that the girls were both physically and mentally tired. I erected the tent, as the ground was too wet and muddy just to lay on, both of them crawled in without a word.

I stayed awake, leaning against a tree, keeping a lookout, I wasn't convinced something wouldn't attack us. My nerves on edge to any movement or sound. Talia, despite her injury, still managed a peaceful smile in her sleep, a gesture that once unnerved us but now brought a sense of comfort, albeit tinged with concern.

In the quiet of the night, amidst the gentle rustling of leaves and distant murmurs of celestial beings, Talia stirred. Her voice, soft and dreamlike, broke the silence. "The stars," she murmured, her words carrying a serene fondness we had come to recognize.

Her love for the stars, a bond we had explored in quieter moments of our journey, surfaced again in her dreams. It was a reminder of her humanity amid the divine tumult that had engulfed us. Akira stirred slightly at the sound of Talia's voice, her brow furrowing in a mix of concern and curiosity. I remained vigilant, listening to the night for any sign of disturbance, but for now, all was calm.

As Talia drifted deeper into her dreams, her smile persisted, a beacon of tranquillity amidst the lingering echoes of Olympus. It was a brief respite, a quiet interlude before the challenges that awaited us at camp and beyond. The three of us had created a bond that none of us would have ever believed could of happened, we weren't just comrades on a quest, that had built a friendship through the trials and challenges we had faced together, it was something more, something that none of us had really had in a long time, a proper sense of belonging, being part of something bigger than ourselves, we had become a family, a strange one I admit, but I knew that whatever happened next we would always have each others backs.

As the night passed, I couldn't rest. I suddenly heard leaves rustling, I stood up swiftly, there was no branch nearby, only small pebbles, so I picked up a handful.

Then without warning a stick snapped behind me, I tried to look menacing but none would have seen anyway, it was super dark.

As I stood up swiftly, clutching my handful of pebbles, my senses on high alert, I strained to discern any movement in the darkness. The rustling leaves hinted at an unseen presence, and another snap of a stick behind me sent a jolt of adrenaline through my veins. Heart pounding, I turned cautiously, squinting into the shadows to catch any sign of what lurked beyond.

"Talia? Akira?" I whispered, hoping it was just one of them moving in their sleep or perhaps a harmless woodland creature. The night remained silent, save for the gentle rustling of leaves and the faint, distant hoots of an owl.

With each step, I edged closer to where I thought the sound had come from, my grip on the pebbles tightening involuntarily. The air crackled faintly with residual energy, a reminder of Zeus's lingering displeasure and the unpredictable nature of Olympus.

Then, from the darkness emerged a figure - a silhouette against the starlit sky. My heart skipped a beat as I prepared to defend myself, pebbles clenched tightly in my hand.

"Who goes there?" I called out, my voice more confident than I felt. The figure hesitated for a moment, then stepped forward into the faint moonlight filtering through the canopy.

It was Talia, her injured shoulder cradled protectively against her side. "Oliver?" she murmured, her voice soft but tinged with concern. "Did I wake you?"

Relief washed over me as I recognised her familiar silhouette. I lowered the pebbles, letting out a nervous laugh. "No, I haven't slept yet," I admitted, my heart still racing from the adrenaline rush. "I thought... never mind."

As Talia approached, I noticed the weariness etched into the lines of her face, contrasting with the serene smile she offered. "Oliver," she began softly, her voice a gentle whisper in the stillness of the night, "you should try to get some sleep. We can't afford to let our guard down, but rest is important."

I nodded, though the thought of sleep seemed a luxury amidst the lingering tension of our encounter with Zeus. "I'll try," I replied, managing a small smile, "but I doubt I'll be able to."

Talia's smile widened slightly, her eyes reflecting the faint starlight above. "I understand," she murmured, her gaze drifting upwards. "The stars always have a way of keeping me awake too. They're mesmerising, aren't they? So vast and full of stories waiting to be told."

Her words stirred a memory from a previous chapter, where we had sat by a campfire and talked about the constellations, sharing stories and dreams beneath the same celestial canopy that now stretched above us. It was a moment of quiet camaraderie, a bond woven by shared experiences and shared awe for the cosmos.

"They really are beautiful," I replied softly, tearing my gaze away from the stars to meet Talia's eyes. Her expression held a mixture of curiosity and warmth, and for a moment, I found myself captivated not just by the stars above but by the person standing before me, my first real friend, except Akira.

Talia tilted her head slightly, studying me with an intensity "You know," she said after a moment, her voice barely above a whisper, "I've never met anyone who looks at the stars quite like you do."

"Well, you've intrigued me," I said.

Talia's eyes sparkled with amusement, a hint of a smile playing on her lips despite the weariness etched into her features. "Intrigued, am I?" she teased gently, her tone softening the edges of our shared tension. "What is it about the stars that captivates you so?"

I chuckled nervously, feeling a flush of embarrassment at being caught off guard. "I guess... I never really noticed them before, but they way you make them sound so much more real," I admitted, my voice quieter now, matching the stillness of the night around us.

"They're like... stories written in the sky, each constellation telling a different tale. It's... peaceful, somehow."

Talia nodded thoughtfully, her gaze drifting upwards once more. "They are storytellers," she agreed softly, her voice carrying a hint of wonder. "Ancient myths and legends woven into the fabric of the cosmos. It's... reassuring, knowing that amidst all this chaos," she gestured vaguely around us, "there's something so constant and timeless."

"Yeah," I murmured in agreement, feeling a sense of connection deepen between us. "Even here, amidst Olympus and all its... drama," I added with a small, nervous chuckle, "the stars remain unchanged."

"They remind us," Talia continued, her voice barely above a whisper now, "that there's more to life than the battles we face. That... even in the darkest moments, there's beauty and stories waiting to be discovered."

Silence settled between us, comfortable and companionable, punctuated only by the soft rustling of leaves and the distant murmurs of Olympus. It was a moment of respite, a chance to breathe amidst the turmoil that had defined our journey so far.

Akira stirred nearby, her soft snoring a reminder of her presence. Talia glanced back at her, a fond smile playing on her lips before she turned her attention back to me. "Thank you, Oliver," she said sincerely, her eyes searching mine. "For standing up for us... for me. Against Zeus."

I swallowed, feeling a lump form in my throat at her gratitude. "I... I couldn't just stand by," I replied quietly, my gaze dropping briefly before meeting hers again. "You're my... friend, Talia, and... friends look out for each other, right? I mean if we are friends... I've never really had any before. I'll just go to bed," of course I was messing this up, the first time I had a real friend and I was messing it up.

As Talia looked at me, her expression softened with understanding. "You're doing just fine, Oliver," she reassured me gently. "Being a friend means being there, even when things are tough or uncertain. It's about standing up for each other, even against powerful odds." Her smile grew warmer. "And you've already proven yourself more than capable of that."

I felt a wave of relief wash over me at her words, a weight lifting from my shoulders. Talia's kindness and patience were reassuring, reminding me that friendship wasn't about being perfect but about being there, through thick and thin.

"Thanks, Talia," I replied, managing a small smile. "I'm glad you're here."

Akira stirred again, mumbling something in her sleep. Talia chuckled softly, glancing at her with affection. "And Akira too," she added fondly, "we make quite a team, don't we?"

I nodded, feeling a sense of camaraderie that hadn't fully formed until this moment. "Yeah, we do. We're a pretty unconventional team, but we make it work."

Talia's smile lingered as she looked up at the stars again. "Maybe that's what makes us stronger," she mused. "Our differences, our unique perspectives - they bring us together in ways we never expected."

As we stood there, a comfortable silence enveloped us, broken only by the occasional rustle of leaves or distant rumble of thunder. The journey back to camp, though fraught with uncertainty, felt more manageable with Talia and Akira by my side. Together, we had faced gods and stood our ground. Whatever challenges lay ahead, I knew we could confront them together.

Eventually, Talia's gaze returned to me. "You should try to get some sleep," she said gently. "I'll keep watch for a while."

I hesitated, but her reassuring smile convinced me. "Alright," I agreed, finding a spot near Akira and settling down.

The ground was hard and uneven, but the exhaustion from the day's events soon overcame my discomfort. As I closed my eyes, the distant murmur of Olympus faded, replaced by the steady rhythm of Akira's breathing and the comforting presence of my friend nearby.

The first light of dawn began to filter through the trees, casting a gentle glow over the forest. I stirred, blinking against the pale light, and noticed Talia and Akira already awake. Talia's shoulder still bore the mark of Zeus's lightning, but she seemed more determined than ever. Akira, though tired, had a renewed sense of purpose in her eyes.

"Morning," Talia greeted, her voice soft but filled with a quiet strength.

"Morning," Akira replied, stretching and shaking off the remnants of sleep. "How's your shoulder?"

Talia shrugged slightly, wincing but managing a small smile. "It'll heal. We have more important things to worry about."

Akira nodded, her expression serious. "We need to get back to camp and regroup. We can't afford to stay out here too long."

We gathered our things, readying ourselves for the journey ahead. The path back to camp stretched before us, a familiar route that now seemed more daunting given the events of the previous night. Yet, there was a newfound determination in our steps, a resolve to face whatever awaited us at camp.

As we walked, the conversation was sparse but meaningful. We shared stories, memories, and plans for what lay ahead. The attachment between us grew stronger with each step, a testament to the trials we had endured together.

The morning light grew brighter, and the forest began to come alive with the sounds of birds and rustling leaves. The tension from the night before began to ease, replaced by a sense of hope.

We didn't know what challenges awaited us back at camp, but we were ready to face them together.

By midday, the forest began to thin, the familiar sights and sounds of camp growing nearer. The distant murmur of voices and the smell of wood smoke were welcoming, a promise of safety, rest and a good meal. My stomach thinks my throat has been cut after living off beef jerky and forest nuts.

As we approached the barrier to the camp and recited the password, ánoixe sousámi, the campers greeted us with a mixture of surprise and excitement. Word of our confrontation with Zeus had spread, and whispers of our bravery filled the air. Athena, the camp's matronly figure, approached us with open arms.

"You've made it back," she said, her voice warm and filled with pride, "come, let's tend to your wounds and hear your tale."

The campers gathered around, eager to hear about our journey. As we recounted our story, the campfire crackled and popped, the flames dancing in the late afternoon light. Athena's presence was a comforting one, her wisdom and kindness a balm to our weary souls.

Talia's injury was tended to with care, the burn from Zeus's lightning treated with a salve that glowed faintly under Athena's touch. Akira's nerves, still frayed from the confrontation, were soothed by Athena's gentle words and the supportive murmurs of our fellow campers.

That night after most people went to bed we pulled Athena aside, "Athena, we should probably tell you that Nemesis warned us about something, a great danger that affects gods and mortals alike, something that could threaten all our lives."

"Do you know what she meant by that?" Athena asked, trying to hide her worried expression but failing miserably.

"No, but we could tell Nemesis was really scared, we thought we should let you know."

"Thank you, children, you should go and rest now, we are all very proud of you, Hera has managed to dampen Zeus's electric temper to the best of her abilities, Nyx seems satisfied with the safe return, if Nemesis, so thank you for saving us all from eternal night."

As the sun dipped below the horizon, casting the camp in a warm, golden glow, a sense of peace settled over us. We had faced gods and stood our ground, emerging not unscathed but undeniably stronger.

That night, under the same stars that had watched over us throughout our journey, we found a sense of belonging. Together, we had faced the wrath of the divine and emerged united, our bonds forged in the crucible of adversity. The path ahead was still uncertain, but for now, we had each other, and that was enough.

As I settled into my bedroll, the familiar sounds of camp life surrounding me, I felt a profound sense of gratitude. For my friends, for the courage we had found within ourselves, and for the stars that continued to guide us, reminding us that even in the darkest of times, there was light and hope and I fell into a deep sleep.

- Chapter 18 -

New Friends and a Tale

Back at camp, the buzz of daily activities and the lively chatter of campers resonated the air, providing an inviting presence compared to the tension of Olympus. The familiar sights and sounds brought a sense of normalcy, a reprieve from the divine chaos we had faced. Yet, there was an undercurrent of change - whispers about our confrontation with Zeus, and speculation about our bond with Talia.

As we re-entered the campgrounds, the campers eyed us with a mixture of curiosity and wariness. Akira, always the more outgoing of the three of us, waved at a few familiar faces, receiving friendly nods in return. She had quickly integrated into the camp community, her natural charisma winning her friends like Leslie Hernandez and Sae De Jong. Leslie, with her fiery red hair and bright blue eyes, and Sae, with her striking pink hair and grey eyes were often seen at Akira's side, sharing laughs and stories.

Leslie and Sae greeted us warmly. "Hey, welcome back!" Leslie called out, her eyes sparkling with genuine happiness. "How was the trip to Olympus?"

"Eventful," Akira replied with a grin, exchanging a knowing look with me.

Sae nudged Akira playfully. "You'll have to tell us everything later, we've missed you."

It was amazing how many people liked you when you got back from a successful quest.

As Akira engaged in animated conversation with her friends, I couldn't help but feel a twinge of envy at how easily she connected with others. I stayed a step behind, offering polite nods and smiles to those who acknowledged me. My thoughts wandered to Talia, who had slipped quietly into the girls' cabin, avoiding the curious stares of the other campers.

I wandered towards the boys' cabin, trying to blend into the background. I wasn't particularly close with anyone yet. My interactions with the other campers were limited, and I often found myself feeling like an outsider. I sat on the steps of the cabin, watching the hustle and bustle of camp life.

Marcus, Talia's half-brother, walked past, his light brown skin glowing under the midday sun. He glanced at me briefly before continuing on his way, his expression indifferent. Despite sharing a sibling bond with Talia, he seemed to avoid her just as much as the other campers did. I made a mental note to ask Talia more about her brother, though he never really came up in conversation on the quest.

Barnabas Wallaby, another camper with a more muscular build and a perpetually serious expression, approached me. "Hey, Oliver," he greeted, his tone neutral, "heard you stood up to Zeus."

I nodded, unsure of how to respond. "Yeah, it was... intense."

Barnabas studied me for a moment before offering a slight nod of approval. "Takes guts, just watch your back, alright?"

"Thanks," I replied, appreciating the gesture, though it did little to ease my anxiety. If anything, it worried me more.

As the day wore on, I found myself gravitating towards the edges of camp activities, observing rather than participating. It was a habit I had developed over time, keeping my distance, and staying out of trouble. Yet, I couldn't shake the feeling that things were changing, that my role within this camp and within this group was evolving.

In the evening, a campfire was lit in the central clearing. The campers gathered around, sharing stories and laughter. I sat a little away from the main group, close enough to feel the warmth of the fire but far enough to remain on the periphery. Akira, Leslie, and Sae sat together, their laughter and animated conversation a comforting backdrop.

I noticed Talia standing at the edge of the clearing, her eyes reflecting the flickering flames. She hesitated before making her way to the fire, choosing a spot a little away from the others. The campers' reactions were mixed, some curious, some wary. Her ever-present smile, a mask for her past pain, still unsettled many who didn't understand it.

Deciding to bridge the gap, I stood up and walked over to her, sitting down beside her. She looked surprised but grateful. "Hey, Talia," I greeted softly.

"Hey, Oliver," she replied, her voice barely audible over the crackling fire, "you didn't have to sit here, you know."

I shrugged, offering her a small smile. "I wanted to, we're friends, right?"

Talia's smile widened, a hint of genuine warmth breaking through. "Yeah, we are."

We sat in comfortable silence for a while, watching the flames dance.

Eventually, Akira noticed us and waved us over. "Come on, you two! Join us!"

I glanced at Talia, who hesitated for a moment before nodding. Together, we moved closer to the fire, integrating ourselves into the larger group. Leslie and Sae made room for us, their friendly smiles easing the transition.

As the evening wore on, stories of bravery and adventure were shared, with Akira recounting our encounter with Zeus in vivid detail. The campers listened with rapt attention, their expressions a mix of awe and disbelief. I noticed Marcus sitting nearby, his gaze occasionally flickering to Talia with a mix of curiosity and something else, perhaps regret or guilt.

When the stories shifted to lighter topics, the atmosphere relaxed. Talia leaned towards me, her voice low. "Thank you for sticking by me, Oliver, it means a lot."

I met her gaze, feeling a sense of companionship and trust. "Of course, Talia. We're in this together."

As the campfire crackled and conversations wound down, a hush fell over the group. Akira, Leslie, and Sae exchanged knowing glances, then turned to Talia and me with genuine admiration in their eyes.

"You guys are so brave," Leslie said earnestly, her voice filled with awe. "Taking on Zeus like that? Not many would have had the guts."

Sae nodded emphatically. "Yeah, seriously! And Talia, that lightning strike... You're like, super tough."

Akira chimed in with a playful grin. "Hey, Oliver, aren't we lucky to have Talia?"

Talia blushed slightly at the praise, her usual modesty tempered by a grateful smile, though her shock was evident. "Thank you, all of you," she replied softly. "It means a lot."

I felt a swell of pride mixed with humility at their words. "Yeah," I added, finding my voice amidst the admiration, "we make a good team."

The campers nodded in agreement, murmuring their approval as they began to disperse for the night. Akira threw an arm around my shoulder, Leslie and Sae, joining in the camaraderie. Talia stood beside us, her presence a quiet anchor amidst the newfound friendships.

As we made our way back to our respective cabins, I couldn't shake the warmth that filled me. Despite the uncertainties ahead, I knew one thing for certain: with friends like Akira and Talia, and newfound allies like Leslie and Sae, I was exactly where I needed to be.

As the night wore on, the conversation shifted from recounting our meeting with Zeus to lighter topics, camp gossip, past adventures, and shared interests. Akira's infectious laughter rang out frequently, punctuating the stories with her vibrant personality. Leslie and Sae, always quick with a joke or an insightful comment, seamlessly integrated me into their circle, making me feel more included than I had in a long time.

Beside me, Talia sat quietly, her usual serene demeanour softened by the flickering firelight. She listened attentively to the conversations around her, occasionally contributing a thoughtful remark or sharing a fond memory of her own. Despite the lingering glances and whispered murmurs from some of the campers, she remained composed, her gentle smile unwavering.

Marcus, Talia's half-brother, sat across the fire, his expression guarded yet contemplative. I caught his gaze on several occasions, his eyes lingering on Talia with a mix of regret and admiration. It was clear that their relationship carried its own complexities, woven with threads of familial duty and unspoken history.

Akira leaned in, her voice lowered conspiratorially as she shared a humorous anecdote from the past quest. Leslie and Sae erupted into laughter, their faces alight with genuine joy. Talia chuckled softly beside me, her eyes reflecting the dancing flames as she glanced around at our group.

- Chapter 19 -

A Camp Dance

The camp buzzed with excitement as the day unfolded, settling into a rhythm of activities and training sessions. The events of Olympus still lingered in the air, a constant reminder of the challenges we had faced and the bonds that had strengthened in adversity. As afternoon stretched into evening, a sense of anticipation rippled through the campgrounds.

It was during breakfast, amidst the chatter and clatter of utensils, that Athena herself made an announcement. Standing at the head of the dining pavilion, her presence commanded attention. Her voice, clear and authoritative, cut through the noise.

"Campers," she began, her stormy eyes scanning the gathered faces with a mix of warmth and solemnity, "in light of recent events and to celebrate the resilience shown by our demigods, I am pleased to announce that there will be a dance held this evening, for anyone who would like to attend."

A ripple of surprise and excitement swept through the pavilion. Whispers and murmurs erupted as campers exchanged curious glances.

We found out a dance was a rare treat at Camp, usually reserved for special occasions or celebrations.

"The dance will commence after nightfall," Athena continued, her gaze settling briefly on each table. "I encourage all of you to attend, to unwind and enjoy each other's company. It is a chance for unity, amidst the trials we face both within and beyond these borders."

With those words, Athena stepped back, her presence lingering in the charged atmosphere.

The campers erupted into a mixture of cheers and enthusiastic conversations. Plans were quickly made, alliances forged for the upcoming evening. People were chatting about what they were going to wear and who was going with who.

At the Athena table, where Sae sat with her siblings and cabin-mates, there was an undercurrent of excitement. Sae's grey eyes sparkled with anticipation as she turned to Akira and Leslie, her voice filled with enthusiasm. "We have to go, it'll be so much fun!"

Akira grinned, nodding in agreement. "Definitely! A chance to relax and let loose after everything."

Meanwhile, at the Nemesis table, Talia listened quietly to the buzz around her. Her expression was thoughtful, her gaze drifting to where I sat. Despite the reserved nature of Nemesis campers, there was a hint of curiosity in her eyes, a silent invitation.

As for me, sitting with my fellow Zeus campers, the prospect of a dance felt both thrilling and daunting. I glanced around at the lively discussions, feeling a sense of solidarity but also a twinge of uncertainty. Would I belong there, amidst the revelry and celebration? I didn't know how to dance, we never had lessons at boarding school.

The evening approached swiftly, the sun sinking below the horizon in a blaze of oranges and pinks. Campers prepared themselves, donning their best attire or simply opting for a more casual approach. Akira, ever the fashion enthusiast, had managed to procure a light pink dress for the occasion, her excitement was obvious, as she twirled in front of the mirror.

Talia, true to her nature, chose a simple yet elegant purple dress that complemented her calm demeanour. Her smile was serene as she adjusted her injured shoulder, preparing herself for the evening ahead.

And then there was me, opting for a comfortable shirt and jeans, feeling slightly out of place amidst the preparations. Akira noticed my hesitation and flashed me an encouraging smile.

"You look great, Oliver. Trust me, you'll fit right in."

As the hour of the dance approached, the campfire crackled softly in the gathering dusk. Music floated through the air, mingling with laughter and excited chatter. Campers began to gather at the clearing designated for the dance, the atmosphere charged with anticipation and the promise of a night to remember.

Akira, Leslie, and Sae found each other amidst the growing crowd, their laughter infectious as they linked arms. Talia stood nearby, her gaze thoughtful as she observed the scene unfolding before her. She glanced over at me, a small smile playing on her lips, not her usual fake smile, a genuine one, the smile I had only seen a few times over the past few weeks.

"Are you coming, Oliver?" Talia asked gently, her voice carrying above the background noise. "As friends?"

I hesitated for a moment, feeling a rush of gratitude for her invitation. "Yeah," I replied with a smile, my nerves easing at her reassuring presence. "I'll join you."

With that decision made, we joined the throng of campers converging on the dance floor. The music swelled, drawing us into its rhythm. The night was alive with energy and laughter, a celebration of resilience and alliances.

Under the starlit sky, surrounded by new friends made, I found myself letting go of the worries that had plagued me since the beginning of the quest. The dance became a moment of freedom, a chance to be a kid for a second.

Akira spun under the twinkling lights, her laughter blending with the music. Leslie and Sae joined in, their movements fluid and joyful. Talia danced with a quiet grace, her eyes reflecting the flickering campfire and the stars above.

And as for me, I found my rhythm alongside them, stepping out of my comfort zone and into a night filled with unexpected joy. The dance floor became a canvas where worries faded and friendships flourished, where the echoes of Olympus were drowned out by laughter and enjoyment.

As the evening wore on, amidst the merriment and music, I realised that I had found more than just friends at Camp. I had found a new family, a diverse, resilient family thrown together by a common connection of being demigods.

Underneath the canopy of stars, as the campfire crackled and the music played on, I knew that this dance marked not just a celebration, but a testament to our unity and the unwavering spirit that defined us as demigods of Camp. And so, we danced into the night, our steps echoing the journey that had brought us together, embracing the moments of joy that illuminated our path forward.

As the dance drew to a close, we gathered around the dwindling campfire, the embers casting a warm glow on our faces. The night had been a resounding success, we shared stories and laughter, our voices blending harmoniously in the quiet of the night.

In that moment, as I looked around at my fellow campers, I felt a profound sense of belonging. Camp wasn't just a place where demigods trained and faced challenges, it was a sanctuary where friendships blossomed and memories were made. The dance had brought us closer, forging connections that would endure long after the music faded and the stars dimmed.

As I finally bid goodnight to my friends and retreated to my cabin, the echoes of laughter and music lingered in my mind. I felt like I finally found my home.

- Chapter 20 -

The Half Term Holidays

It had been a week since we had arrived back, and it was only a few days until the half term holidays. Talia was going to stay with her mother, Nemesis, and Nyx for a while, to reunite, her brother was going to join them for a few days as well, to try to rekindle their relationships.

Akira pondered aloud as we walked by the lake one evening, the sun setting in a blaze of reds and purples over the horizon. "Do you think we should go back?" she asked, her voice tinged with uncertainty.

"Do you mean HollowHead High?" I remarked with a shocked reaction.

"Yes, I do, it's an important couple of years in my education and I don't want to fall behind. I know it sounds absurd, considering everything," said Akira.

"It's bonkers, we've never fitted in there, we spent our whole life being bullied and constantly looking over our shoulders waiting for Demi, Brooklyn and their pose. I don't want to leave here, think of the things we've already accomplished and the new friends we've made. Please Akira, can we not stay here?" I pleaded.

I kicked a pebble into the water, watching the ripples spread.

She nodded thoughtfully. "Yeah, I get that, but what about our studies? What about-"

Her words were interrupted by the sudden appearance of Athena walking towards us.

"Akira, Oliver," she greeted us warmly, her voice a steady reassurance amidst our uncertainty. "I've heard you're considering your options for the holidays."

I exchanged a glance with Akira, unsure of how much Athena knew about our predicament. "Yeah," I replied tentatively, "we're not sure if we should go back to school or stay here."

"It's normal for new campers to feel unsure about staying, some people leave for the holidays, some people leave forever, some people stay until they're adults.

Athena regarded us with a thoughtful expression, her eyes seeming to pierce through our uncertainties. "Camp offers a unique environment for demigods to grow and train, but the decision ultimately rests with each camper and their personal journey," she said, her voice measured yet encouraging. "There is no right or wrong choice, only what feels right for you. But personally I would like you to stay here."

Akira nodded, her brow furrowed in contemplation. "I just don't know if going back to school will feel the same after everything we've experienced here," she admitted, her voice tinged with hesitation.

"It's natural to feel that way," Athena acknowledged, her tone gentle, "attending school provides a different kind of learning and social environment, one that is valuable in its own right. However, Camp offers a sense of community and understanding that may be harder to find elsewhere."

I thought back over the past few weeks, about

the quest and the few days spent at camp, I had felt more at home here than I had ever felt at school. I remembered Talia's words, we learnt normal things at camp, maths, English, geography. But we also learnt things that could be useful. Sword fighting, archery, self defence classes, agility classes and many more.

As I reflected on Athena's words and the contrasting environments of school and camp, I realised how much more Camp offered beyond traditional education. Here, amidst the trials and adventures, we weren't just learning academic subjects; we were honing skills crucial for survival in a world fraught with mythological challenges. It was a catalyst for personal growth and empowerment and embracing our new identities as demigods and finding our place in the world that so often we felt at odds with.

"Akira, Oliver," Athena continued, her voice carrying a weight of understanding. "Your experiences here have been unique, shaping not just your abilities but also your perspectives. It's natural to feel torn between the familiarity of school and the newfound sense of belonging at Camp."

Akira nodded, her expression thoughtful. "I suppose we have to weigh what's important to us," she mused, her gaze drifting across the tranquil lake, "school taught us one set of skills, but Camp has taught us so much more about ourselves and our potential."

"Athena," I ventured, seeking guidance amidst my swirling thoughts, "what if we choose to stay at camp for the holidays? Will it hinder our academic progress?"

The goddess regarded me with a reassuring smile. "Camp offers a comprehensive education that encompasses both traditional subjects, normal exams and specialised training," she explained. "Staying here allows you to continue honing your unique abilities while fostering resilience and community among your peers."

Her words resonated deeply, reaffirming my growing conviction that Camp was where I belonged. It wasn't just about academic advancement anymore; it was about embracing a lifestyle that nurtured my strengths and prepared me for the challenges ahead.

"Akira," I said, turning to her with newfound

clarity, "I think I've made my decision. I want to stay at Camp."

She met my gaze, a mix of relief and determination shining in her eyes. "Me too," she replied, her voice steady, "I don't think I'm ready to go back to a place where I never truly felt like I belonged."

With our decision made, a weight lifted from my shoulders, replaced by a sense of purpose and excitement for the holidays ahead. Camp had become more than just a place of training and quests; it was our home.

"As you embark on this next phase of your journey," Athena said, her voice carrying a note of pride, "remember that Camp will continue to support your growth, both as demigods and as individuals."

And so, as the half term holidays commenced and camp quieted with the departure of some and the stay of others, Akira and I settled into a routine of rigorous training, insightful lessons.

As we immersed ourselves in activities that ranged from sword fighting to mythology studies, I felt a sense of fulfilment that I had never experienced in the confines of a classroom.

The knowledge gained here wasn't confined to textbooks; it was practical, empowering, and deeply rooted in the rich tapestry of Greek mythology that surrounded us. Apparently the half term holidays at camp were two weeks instead of one, thanks to the gods.

It had only been a week of the holidays when two unexpected guests had arrived, walking into camp hand in hand. There were many gasps and whispers spreading around.

"I can't believe it," Rebecca Cooper, daughter of Hecate whispered to Eris's son, Tim, "after all these years."

Akira and I pushed our way to the front. Who were these people? Why was everyone so surprised?

When we got to the front, Akira stopped suddenly, making me bump into her.

"Ouch!" I said, rubbing my head. I stood up and peeked around her. I saw a girl, messy blonde hair, piercing blue eyes and vitiligo. It was Jane, the girl we met before we got on the train at the very start of our quest.

"Hello, Oliver, Akira," Jane nodded to us, Skafos right behind her.

"Uhh... hi," I said.

"We've got some news, and we are going to need you, Akira and Talia more than ever. Are you ready for another battle of the Gods?" Skafos asked in her thick Italian accent.

Everyone was looking at us now. Great! Just what we needed, more attention.

The End.

About the Author
Hayley Mae Masters

Hayley Mae Masters is a twelve-year-old with a passion for creativity and storytelling. Her favourite school subjects are English and Drama, where she thrives in expressing her ideas and imagination. In her spare time, Hayley enjoys reading, writing, travelling and drawing.

From a very young age, Hayley has always loved writing short stories, delving into history, and getting lost in books. Growing up in Dubai, she has had the unique opportunity to socialise within a multicultural society, allowing her to learn about and share in her friends' diverse cultures and celebrations. This experience has educated her on different perspectives and broadened her understanding of the world.

Hayley has also been fortunate to travel to various countries, which has enriched her experiences and provided inspiration for her writing. The stories and cultures she has encountered on her travels have deeply influenced her work, allowing her to adapt these experiences into her storytelling.

Hayley dreams of becoming an author and actress when she grows up. She aspires to use her writing to promote a world where people of all nationalities are seen as one, without prejudice, and where everyone is treated equally and with respect.

+++++

Follow Hayley's publishing journey here,

www.youngauthoracademy.com/hayley

Scan Me
(with your camera phone)

Printed in Great Britain
by Amazon